Hey Shana!
Thanks Much and
I hope you
Came about how
ignoring her
Stubbins!
Emma Southee

MW01234572

VAMPIRE REBORN

A Tamson Huntress Story

EMMA SOUTHEE

PublishAmerica
Baltimore

First printing

All characters in this book are fictitious, and any resemblance to real persons, living or dead, is coincidental.

PublishAmerica has allowed this work to remain exactly as the author intended, verbatim, without editorial input.

Hardcover 978-1-4512-8615-1
Softcover 978-1-4512-8516-8
PUBLISHED BY PUBLISHAMERICA, LLLP
www.publishamerica.com
Baltimore

Printed in the United States of America

I would like to thank my husband Rob, who stood by me even when he would be ignored while I wrote. To Tiff for keeping my spirits up, refilling my coffee and helping me keep stress at bay. Thanks to all my friends and family that kept asking me about my books so I would have to keep going. Special thanks go out to my mom who not only supports me but proofread the rough first copy even though this book is not the genre she likes. Big thanks go to Amy for turning me on to vampires back in middle school when I was still obsessed with witches, hope you like the changes I made from that first draft!

I would also like to thank PublishAmerica officially for giving Tamson this chance. She has been living in my head for so long it's wonderful to see her take shape.

Chapter 1
The End Begins

I feign a shiver and pull my light brown pea coat closer around
me in the dark doorway as I wait for a man to come to me. The
cream scarf tight around my face does not hide me from the cold
that has everyone else running for shelter. It does however hide my
pale face from view. Keeping my straight jaw and curved lips
concealed from view so no one can remark on them later.

It's not just that my jaw is straight, but you can see the bone
structure. Strong straight lines with no whisper of blemish, mixed
with the length and thinness of my neck and chin, set against pale
white skin tend to emphasize lips that are by contrast full, curved
and rich with color. When your lips are as red as an apple off the tree
with a natural shine like dew, you don't need extra emphasis from
your features.

Actually girl, if you weren't out here playing mouse you would
like the emphasis, it's just you're in a weird situation where being a
one of a kind makes life hard.

I don't hide my features to avoid stares and comments. If things
were different I may even flaunt my face around. I hide them so no
whispered conversations reach the ears of the one person in the
world who would know that I was the one they had seen.

My deep red hair with highlights both light and dark made a color that was also hard to pass over without notice. I had tried hair dye, and it just washes out. My hair thinks it's perfect and will not absorb anything into it.

So as well as the scarf for my face, my waist length hair was pulled up in a tight braid and wrapped around under a big knit hat that matched the scarf. Other then the blue jeans, I was dressed like I was modeling a new fashion line of winter chic. I wasn't, but it helped me blend in without using any energy to look unremarkable. I felt my hunter getting close and was trying hard not to use any power for fear it would bring him closer faster.

For now though, I was not waiting for him. Adam would find me later if I didn't leave this city, but tonight he's not close enough. So I need to get something to eat and begin to finish up my years of planning and training. That's why I'm standing here wasting time trying to look cold while I wait for some man to find me. If I wasn't so picky I would already be sitting in my apartment but a girl has to have standards. Granted most standards are for the bigger better man but I won't let myself partake of anything good.

So I look around waiting for someone who is tainted. It doesn't take long. It never does in this city, in this neighborhood. Which I guess is good for a self repentant vampire, but what does that say of humanity.

I don't have time to contemplate that again tonight though, I spot my meal. A man leaves a bar and starts walking my way. He smells of corruption. Not just the alcohol, but something inside him has twisted. He'll make a fine meal. He'll taste awful, but when only innocents are delicious, I'll pass thank you very much.

He's so close, but still doesn't see me. He leans on a wall and starts to fall. Bumps his head on a brick then straightens out and walks too purposefully. He was trying with all his might to walk like he wasn't full to the eyes with vodka martinis, even though he still had a toothpick in his hands. Maybe he wasn't sure enough of himself to put something so sharp in his mouth while he focused so hard on just moving his feet.

It didn't matter; a toothpick won't hurt my skin when mascara won't even stay on my lashes. He walks right by me and stares straight ahead. If he had seen me; he didn't see me as a threat, but I was guessing he hadn't seen me because he was too preoccupied making his body listen.

I lean out of the doorway and turn fast, pushing him into the alley and shadows. Touching so lightly but precisely that it probably felt like wind to him, and a stumble. He tries to get up and ends up spinning in a circle, grabbing his head, falling to his butt on some trash bags and hitting his head on the bricks behind him. I didn't mean for all that, but it works out. His lungs and heart are still going, and now that he's passed out I don't have to worry about wasting energy to keep him still and unseeing or feeling while I feed.

He didn't have any bleeding wounds, so I pull out my small knife. I look around for an excuse he will be able to believe and see a few boards with nails and sharp edges near his head level while sitting. That'll do I guess.

Pulling my scarf off my mouth I breathe in the night air and commit myself once again. I make a sharp cup across his neck and bend to the lifeblood that sustains and revolts me. When I feel I have enough to keep me going for tonight I lift my head and take a deep breath.

I use the knife to smear blood along the boards and one of the nails. Leaning him closer towards them and placing a compulsion for him to wake up in a few minutes. I always make it look like they hurt themselves accidentally. I hope that it'll make them think twice about their way of life. Sadly though, I have found a few of my victims later and none I had found seemed to change.

I leave him in the alley and spend a little energy to blur my image. I make my way back to my apartment building and glance around as I quickly sneak in. I walk into my apartment and wish once more that

I had a cat. I had one ages ago, but it was hard to change lives and make the cat deal. It was also harder to hide it with power. Constant energy spent made it easier for Adam to track me.

Not for long I thought as I look across the little dining room to the new computer on my desk. I had never used one before but I don't like writing a lot with pens. Even eternal fingers hurt after hours of scratching paper. I had bought it for one reason and one only.

I was tired of hiding. I realized that when I started hunting back, I may die. That was an unsettling thought, but there was more. Adam had to be destroyed, and if I died trying to do it, I had to leave an account of my life behind. Hence it was time for an autobiography of sorts.

Keeping all the information to me alone had kept people safe while he was hunting me, but if he defeated me and my knowledge died with me, then everyone would be in danger. Not only that, someone who could hurt him may be able to take over if I failed.

I take the hat off and let the braid roll down. After pushing the power button, I take the scarf off of my face while the computer starts up. The coat gets thrown on the back of the couch and I sit down as the system loads. I sit on the chair and start undoing the braid and pulling my fingers through to loosen the waves away from each other. I pull up the word program and see the tiny cursor blinking at me.

"Where do I start though?" I asked, as if it could tell me. "Everyone says 'start at the beginning' but what beginning should I use?" I thought to myself, 'Do I start at the beginning of time? My first life? My second? My curse or my death? Which death for that matter?'

"How can I explain things so one can understand how I learned everything I know?" I look over to the single photo on the table. It was a picture of a gentleman from the 1800's with his wife and a young daughter. All of them are sitting very straight and smiling just slightly in the fading sepia coloring. "One last family moment before the daughter is married." I touch the glass above their faces slightly. A sadness I hadn't felt in a long time rushes through me. I close my eyes and lean back in my chair. Memories and emotions race through my mind, all fighting for the forefront but only one keeps coming back to me.

"Very well, I'll start with our first meeting. I'll write things down as they happened to me. If someone reads this, they will learn along with me." I start to peck at the keys, going slowly as I try to find the letters. I look up and see the words slowly forming on the screen, as I remember the events that lead to my now cursed life.

Chapter 2
Uninvited Guest

If you are reading this then I most likely died. I am sorry that this fell to your hands but you must read on. You must kill the one who made me. Well, Adam was the one who made me a vampire. He must die, but I alone know all of the reasons why.

What you are reading will contain my life story, and in it, his personality. His sins, corruption, and pure evilness will show through my life. Once you have read this, you will know me, and in that, you will know him. You will know why he must die.

I am going to write a bit about myself, my mortal life. It is not the most educational way to impart my knowledge, but I think knowing me, and learning the way I learned will help.

It was 1883 and I was turning 16 years old. I stood on the landing between the downstairs Hall and the upstairs corridor of my father's house. I was staring at the woman in the mirror that had stolen my face. At least that's how I felt.

It was my Coming of Age Debut ball. My father was not nobility, but we were wealthy. Wealthy enough that, as I was told, some men would seek my hand for nothing other than a business connection, with no thought to feelings. I tried not to think that downstairs there were men who would be looking at me as a possible business expense. I tried to focus on having fun at my very first ball. Earlier in the night I had been sitting in my dressing room and my nurse and mother were painting my face and pulling my hair. After squeezing into a dress that had been made just for tonight, I was rushed out to the hallway with etiquette reminders and told to wait until father announced me.

So there I stood looking in the mirror. Mother had pulled most of my hair into a bun in the back of my head. She had curled ringlets into the front of my face so they hung down in front of my ears to my shoulders. In the back she had made them touch my shoulders at the edges but slowly got longer until the Ringlets at the center of my back almost touched my waist. I loved my hair but had never seen it so beautifully done. My hair flowed with me when I turned, but returned to its place when I stopped. The slow point to my lower back made my waist seem smaller. Somehow it also looked feminine and young, while proud and grown at once.

My hair amazed me, but not as much as the dress. The dress was worth staring at, even if I wasn't in it. It was deep green, and cut so low that I felt naked. Mother assured me that it was proper and fashionable, and that no one would take notice. I was still shocked. I thought if no one would notice then why couldn't I have a higher collar like hers, but I did not ask.

There was nothing on my shoulders, the lace sleeves cuffed my arm and went straight across my chest to the other sleeve. The lace went across what of my chest was covered, layered over the soft velvet of the bodice.

The bodice pushed what little I had up and held it in place, while pulling my waist as tiny as it could go. When I had first seen it I thought I would be uncomfortable, but it wasn't much smaller than the dinner one I had worn before, so I could handle it.

My silk skirts were the same emerald green and were slightly bumped out in the back so my hair almost touched them when I looked up. My skirts went all the way to the tip of my shoes, so when I walked I did not walk on them, but the illusion was they touched the floor. Only the smallest of hoops allowed the tips of my light green boots to be seen when I stepped.

I turned side to side and watched the skirts flow and my hair bouncing and could not believe it was me that I was looking at.

I could already hear people who were getting here at the very beginning downstairs. I had been given a small dinner so I would not be hungry throughout the night. Mother assured me that I would not want to eat in front of people the first time they saw me.

"It's not that it's unladylike, but when first meeting, one does not want to think of chewing and digesting food." She had told me when I asked. I had gone to the washroom before putting on the dress and all that was left was for her to tell Father I was ready.

After that he would bring everyone to the Hall, he would announce me and the green curtains hung atop our stairs would open to reveal me standing at the top. I was to walk down, trailing just my fingertips on the handrail, without looking down. Smile out to the crowd with unwavering grace. Father would take my hand and then I was to interact with the guests.

The problem was once I saw myself I forgot almost everything. I had trouble remembering what dance went to what song. How I was to address certain people. I was still staring at myself and wondering what I was going to do, when Mother came from upstairs.

Her dress was a very simple yet elegant light blue. She had actual sleeves on hers, and a neck line that covered her chest and shoulders. I loved my dress but silently wished it was made a bit more like hers just so I would feel covered.

"You look beautiful. I cannot believe how you have grown." She came down to the landing and held her hands out for me. I went to her and put my fingers in her hands as she pulled me into a small hug. "Do not worry. This is your night, no one else's. It may lead to a new life, or it may not, but do not worry about that. Enjoy this night." She spoke happily and smiled but her eyes were shining. Her smile pulled down just a little at the corners.

"Mother, I am worried though, what if I do not like anyone here. If a man here does ask for my hand, I am scared I won't be happy." Until I said it aloud I didn't even know that it was bothering me. "That is not a concern for tonight, dear. You should always know that, no matter what happens, you will always be my little girl. Your father and I care for you very much, and would never see you unhappy." She pulled me close again without messing our dresses, "Now I will go tell your Father we have finished and when he believes all are here he will call for you." She let go and rushed down without looking at me. But to this day I still think I saw her wipe away a tear.

I stood there a little bit longer, and then sat down on the chair by the mirror. If I was to be dancing and walking around I wanted to rest my feet first. The sound of voices got a bit louder as more arrived and were shown to the ballroom. My stomach was doing flips as I tried to calm down and breathe

'Would he be here' I thought. 'Is the man who will one day be my husband here tonight?' I was going crazy with my own thoughts when I heard

Yes. I am here.

I looked up and around but saw no one. I peeked around the edge of the curtains at everyone down the stairs and all were talking cheerfully.

'I must be going crazy.' I thought to myself.

No my darling you are fine

I could hear my father starting the speech announcing me. I didn't catch the words as he hushed the crowd. I was making sure my dress looked right; I made sure that my hair was in position. As I was straightening up and getting ready for the curtain to open when a whisper passed my ear again.

You have never looked bad a day in your life, stop worrying and just come find me

I tried so hard to keep a smile on my face but was worried. Where was this voice coming from, was there someone upstairs teasing me? Was I imagining things? I heard my father words only in pieces for the voice kept interrupting him.

"For coming tonight…"

No problem I would not miss it for the world

"The proudest moment in my life…"

And in mine

"The pleasure of announcing."

The pleasure of receiving

I didn't even hear my father speak my name but the curtains were opening so I stood straight and smiled. Father turned to me and held up a hand, my cue to start walking down the stairs. I kept my head up and smiled out over the crowd as I was shown, glancing down only with my eyes to check my footing, gliding my fingertips on the rail but not grasping with my hand.

You are beautiful

I kept smiling as my father held his hand up for mine. He took my fingers and stood with me as everyone clapped. He pulled me into a very small hug and my mother came over to stand with us.

"Thank you all so much for joining us this evening" I said in as hostess-like voice as I could manage. They all clapped as my father walked me into the ballroom with mother beside me and they followed.

All I could think of though, was the voice.

Wouldn't have missed this night for anything dearest

We entered the ball room and as others followed the music started. My father started the dance with me. Everyone watched and I could see a few mothers nudging their boys to walk forward. I smiled a little at their shyness. At least I wasn't the only one nervous.

Father Looked down and smiled at me. "It is good to see you

smile. You look so beautiful, like your mother. I hope you enjoy tonight."

"I will try Father." I replied, "I just hope my feet can stay up with me through the dance" He laughed quietly and mumbled something about his little redheaded jester as one young man finally stepped forward.

As he walked forward, so did my mother. We separated and she took fathers hand as I was passed to the gentleman.

"Good evening "I said as He took my hand.

"Good evening to you, Miss Tamson. My name is Edward."

Mister Eddy better not think he can keep you

I ignored the voice but looked around to see if anyone had heard it. Others had started dancing in pairs. A few young men were dancing with other guests but looking our way. Edward and I spoke for a little while. His father had gone to school with mine and they worked with each other. As he was starting to talk of his own career another young man tapped his shoulder and asked for a dance. Edward bowed to me and handed my hand to the new gentleman.

"I look forward to another dance" and he disappeared into the crowd.

"Hello Miss Tamson, I am Nicholas, you look lovely this evening"

He is a fiend

I danced with Nicholas until the end of the song. He had spent the entire time talking about me, and how nice I looked. Complimenting my father on finding me a dress that made my beauty ever so much more brilliant. I didn't tell him that my mother had found the lady and helped design it. I just smiled and thought, 'This is one of those men who see me as a business expense and something to look pretty on his arm.'

As the dance ended he bowed to me and another young man came up. He looked like he was just a few years older then I and nervous through his smile. I instantly liked him, because he was not overconfident. He bowed and took my hand.

"Good evening Tamson." He said as polite as his shaky voice would allow. "Are you enjoying this evening?"

"Yes, I have been enjoying myself." I answered politely back.

You do not enjoy yourself too much

I smiled past the scolding from nowhere.

"That is wonderful. I hope you are not overwhelmed by everyone here tonight." He seemed sincere and I gave him a real smile, I didn't have to force a smile on my face.

"I hope I am not either. Please, sir, what is your name?"

"Oh my I forgot to introduce myself. I, well, I am Fredrick. I am afraid I do not have any title or family story for you to pretend to be interested in."

I laughed before I could stop myself and then put my face down blushing. A few people round us turned with concern or distaste on their faces, but he just grinned.

"Do not hide your face from a smile or laugh. Happiness should not be kept out of view."

I looked up at him, "No it should not, so I shan't. Fredrick. What is that you do, or are you schooling?"

"Oh not that it matters, but I am in school. My father died when I was younger. Our family was already wealthy from previous generations, and he had been a business man. We own land here and in other regions, so mother is well taken care of. I am learning to take over when I am ready."

"I thought you said you had no story." I joked at him and he smiled with a slight blush, "Is your mother here tonight?"

"Yes. She is over sitting by the veranda window. She has tea with your mother on occasion and thus I was invited tonight" At this he blushed as if he thought he did not deserve to be here. I liked that he blushed so much. It meant he felt things, and did not think himself better than others.

"Well, Fredrick, I for one am pleased that our mothers take tea together or I may never have met you" At this he smiled but mine wavered for all I heard was. *You should not be pleased that he is here, only that I am.* His smile faded and I thought it was due to mine wavering, but he turned and I saw that someone else was tapping him to dance with me.

He politely handed me to the next man, and smiled as I said "It has been a pleasure meeting you." It went on like this for a few more songs. I was passed around to different gentlemen. Each hoping that he would like me enough to court me. Each just as boring as the last and I felt like I had danced with everyone who was not in a dress. All the time I would hear the whispering voice in my ears. No one else seemed to notice so I began to just smile through it.

A few times the voice itself made me smile. The man I would be dancing with would think he was making me smile, so sometimes it worked. The music slowed and my father was holding my hands again.

"Are you enjoying yourself little one?" He asked as we started to move.

"Yes Father." my feet were starting to tire and my responses were getting shorter. I smiled and we danced. He led me over to the side of the dance floor and sat me down on a particularly soft tête-à-tête before the song ended. When I looked up he put up a hand and said, "You rest here. You have been up for awhile and you need to relax. I will be back shortly."

He walked off and a few young men came and asked for a dance, I promised them I would dance later, but right now was waiting for my father. No one wanted to argue with a fathers claim so they all graciously backed away. I was looking out into the crowd, watching them dance. I felt the seat move and turned to see who had sat on the other side.

"Pardon me Miss Tamson." I turned and saw Fredrick holding a glass.

"I saw your Father sitting you down and thought you might like a drink." He handed me the glass and went to leave.

"Thank you so much Fredrick. Please sit by me and talk while I wait for Father to return. Maybe it will stop everyone from asking me to dance." His smile was so wide I thought he might clap his hands but he sat on the other side of the tête-à-tête very calmly.

We sat for a little while, talking about other people here tonight. I enjoyed sitting and leaning on the chair to relax as we talked. We had spoken very briefly about who we knew and didn't know when my father came back.

"Hello Father. This is Fredrick, he brought me a drink" I stood and introduced them.

"Thank you for taking care of my daughter, I was going to ask her to dance, but if you would like to?" He made it a question but walked away, with my glass, before either of us could say anything.

"Well, I guess you better dance with me before someone else takes my hand."

"Oh my lady, you force me to do such a terrible thing as dance with you. You should be ashamed." We laughed quietly as we danced back to the middle of the ballroom.

He was able to dance with me for almost all the song before someone else came to dance with me. I was a little sad to see him go. He at least made me smile and seemed like a friend, the others all seemed too formal. Which I should have been as well, but it wasn't as fun.

As I went to the next man I started hearing the voice again. I hadn't even noticed it had gone.

Sorry I left for awhile. I.

I needed to eat.

I turned around looking again. It was no longer a quiet whisper that seemed inside my head. I felt breath on my shoulders and the words seemed solid. Yet the man I was dancing with was just looking out into the crowd. He did not even notice me, He was just dancing.

I am ready for you now. Come find me.

'I'm going mad' was all I could think, 'How can there be a voice with no real person?'

Oh I am real. You have no idea how real I am. Yet

A few songs went by and I was passed around to dance with more men. Some came back and while I was talking to them I was trying to match their voice to the one I was hearing. I thought one of them must be tricking me somehow. However, each time I would think I may have found someone I would hear him mocking

Not me

Or

Oh that's not me, my pretty miss.

Finally I was tired, exhausted. I looked up at the young man holding my hand and realized I didn't even know his name.

You don't need to worry about HIS name

"I am sorry, sir, but I must ask that I take my leave. I need to rest my feet"

"As you wish, it was my pleasure to dance with you Miss Tamson." I smiled politely and started to walk away with a nod of my head.

I walked to the edge of the dancers, politely refusing a few dance requests on the way. I stepped out onto the veranda. The sun was setting and a chill had started to move in, but I needed air.

You need me

I turned around to see whose hand was on my shoulder but no one was there. I turned back to the yard, eyes wide as I searched the entrances to our garden maze. I could see no one.

"Whose there?" I spoke aloud. Surely this was some game an

older man was playing on me; I was just too naive to understand how it was done. No one answered. I started to feel the cold, and was rubbing my arms and turned to go inside and I gasped.

"Father you startled me, I did not know you were there." He smiled at me from the doorway and lit his pipe. He walked over and we both looked out to the maze.

"Are you still enjoying yourself or are you out here to escape everyone?" He asked me with a smile.

"Oh no I am having a wonderful time." I lied, something felt wrong and this voice was beginning to fill my thoughts. "I just needed some fresh air, I was feeling flushed." I looked over the tops of the bushes. I had played in the maze so often as a child I knew every twist and turn. I had given my nurse quite a scare one time by hiding in the middle and she got lost. I had to go back in to get her and walk her out. She was so happy to be out and laughing that I had come to save her, that I did not get in trouble.

"My child I do not want you to wear yourself out tonight. If you feel like you must rest you can bid goodnight and no one will mind. Women often leave early, do not worry. The men will just sit around talking about unimportant things."

"No father I am fine. I just needed to catch my breath. I will be in momentarily to help hostess the party." I smiled up at him but felt it fade. He just looked at me and smiled back, I still do not know if he saw my face fall or not.

"Well then, if you are enjoying yourself so much, what has made this night pleasant?"

"Well." I thought out loud, "I have never danced so much in one night before. I enjoy hearing how beautiful I am, "I nudged him and he laughed.

"Yes my little jester, you are beautiful tonight. Tomorrow is different and I order you to be my little girl again. Is that understood?"

"Oh yes sir." I joked back. "Let's see. I am pleased to see mother so dressed up, and it's nice to see you at home, but not working."

"Alright, I understand, you like the ball. What I am asking, my little one, Is if any man has been keeping you happy, or if it is just the ball?"

"OH! Is that what you were asking?" I jested at him. We laughed as we often did and both became quiet together as we looked out to the maze again. I don't know if he was looking at it or just over it, but something was drawing me to it.

"Actually Father, I have found one person that keeps a smile on my face." He turned and glanced at me.

"Really? Should I be worried?"

"Oh I should not think so. I met Fredrick. Mother has tea with his mother every so often. He has danced with me twice and brought me the drink. He is nice to talk to."

"Yes I know the lad. He is working hard to finish school so he can come home and take over his father's ventures." He turned and looked at me. "Come, let us go inside. It is getting cool outside and you have nothing to protect you."

I turned and looked back out in the bush maze. Something was making me want to stay outside, though, at the time, I did not know what.

"If it pleases you father, I would like to stay just a moment longer. I promise to come inside before I catch ill. I would like to rest just a moment more." He looked at me and smiled.

"As my little one wishes, so shall I do. I will go and dance with your mother, as it pleases you to see us smiling." He put his arm around my shoulder and kissed the top of my forehead. "You do look beautiful tonight little one. It both saddens me and fills with me with joy to see you so grown."

I hugged him back as much as my corsets would allow and he turned to go inside. I watched him as he got to the door, put out his pipe and looked up at me.

"I will see you inside." He said as he walked in. He left the door open so no chance would I be locked out back and I turned back to the maze. I began walking down to the staircase that led down to the grounds. I stopped and looked back to the doors.

'I should go back in. It is getting cold and I would like to sit in the warmth.' I thought and began walking back when I heard it.

'But I am here now'

I turned to look down the stairs. That breath had been on my ears, I could almost feel someone watching me.

'But where' I thought.

'Come find out' I heard in my head.

'I'm going mad. There's no other explanation. I turned and walked to the doors. My mind set on going inside and ignoring this strange voice that haunted me. Maybe Fredrick would dance with me again, or I might meet someone else who is worth talking to.

"NO!"

I turned back to the maze. That one was real I was sure of it. It was not in my head at all, but spoken into my ears. The wind still echoed with the one word.

Without knowing why I started walking back to the maze. Not using rail or eyes to watch my steps, I simply walked without thinking. I never looked back at the doors.

No one saw them slowly shut in a quiet breeze. The party went on inside, but I was walking into the maze.

Chapter 3
A Maze

At first nothing was wrong, it was my maze. I knew exactly where I was going. I was going to sit down in the middle. An enclave with an old stone bench sat between two ceramic urns with shrubberies. It was a favorite spot of mine when I was a child. My nurse would let me take lessons out there so I would pay attention better. I would go sit on my bench. I would catch my breath and go back to my ball. As I started walking however, something was happening. It seemed like the further in I got, the less the gardener had taken care of the maze. The bushes were growing higher, and branches stuck out. Twice I had to lift my skirts over vines to get past. I went to turn left on a shortcut and it was not there, the branches had grown closed.

I began walking the long way around to the middle and each step the ground was dirtier, the plants wilder. I saw this, I dodged, I would snap twigs with my feet, but I could still see my maze. I was slightly aware of my real maze underlying the vision, but it wasn't real. I knew my maze was trimmed, but I could not walk through the branches my eyes saw. I was confused.

The further I walked the more the overgrown maze started to feel like home. It was familiar, and the trimmed shaped one started to feel odd. I started to feel like the overgrown was right and the memory of a well groomed bushes was wrong. I turned right and was in the center of the maze. But my eyes did not see it.

I saw, instead, a small yard. There were no bushes, but trees. Instead of a stone bench there was a wooden seat, outside a small cottage. I went over and sat on it. Why was I thinking about a stone bench?

I looked down and my dress was gone, but it had never been there. I had always worn homemade clothes. This was my home. I picked up a potted plant and began talking to it as I pulled brown leaves off and tickled the small buds to open.

'Something isn't right though' I thought to myself. 'I was doing something else. I was looking for someone.'

"Were you looking for me?" I turn around and standing by the door to the home was a man. He was familiar to me as the seat I was on, yet I could not name him. My heart smiled as he looked down with a grin.

He stood almost as high as the door. He had made it that way so he would not have to bend over to walk in our home. His light brown hair was loose and it flitted in the breeze around his shoulders. He was also wearing clothes like mine. Thin cotton, wool, and leather. I had made them for him. He came over and stood behind me.

"It will be fine, leave the plant alone" he said as he put his hands on my shoulders.

Then the illusion was gone. The shirt I was wearing had sleeves, but I felt something touching my skin. I looked up and I was sitting on the stone bench, I was in my maze. I was holding a leaf from one of my shrubberies.

There were hands on my shoulders.

I looked up and saw the face of the man from the cottage, but something was different. He was paler, and a bit harsher looking.

His hair was longer, but pulled back from his face. Yet he still seemed familiar to me.

"I told you I was here. I am so glad you came and found me."

"Who are you? Why are you here?" I stuttered out. He had startled me and I realized I was outside, completely alone. "My Father knows I am out here and is waiting for me. I suggest you leave me alone and go away." I was scared. I didn't know why but this man was not right. He should not be here, and I didn't want him touching me.

"Calm down, little one. I would never harm you. You are my wife, even if you do not remember yet." I could not believe my ears.

"Excuse me, Sir, but this is my debut. I am not married and now I will be getting back to my guests." I went to move but his hands were more solid then the stone I sat on. I felt like he could push me right through the bench if he wanted.

"Oh, you will not. Those greedy human males have touched you enough tonight. Now it is my turn." I shivered at the way he spoke. It was not from the cool air. I was scared.

One of his hands started making its way up my neck to my cheek. I tried hard not to move at all, afraid that if I did anything he would hurt me. He let his fingertips trail along and I felt like a snake was upon me. He tilted my face towards him as he smiled down at me and then he tilted my head so I was looking away from him and my hair fell to one side.

"You always had a beautiful face. I missed touching you. You are not quite as grown as I remember you, but it is you." Before I could do or say anything I felt his lips touch my neck. He was kissing me. Something was telling me that it was wrong, that he was not allowed to touch me.   However, my mind did not listen. I let him touch me and for once in my life felt completely happy.

"You will be mine again, but I have to wait." He said. "Before I go however, I want to make doubly sure you are she. So just relax and enjoy this."

I didn't worry, I relaxed. I felt a slight pain, like he had bit me, but then I was seeing the small home again. I had put the plant down and was working with some small seeds. I turned to the left and waved my hand with my fingers open. Four small lines opened in the dirt. I began spreading the seeds through the lines, when the home disappeared and I was back in my maze. He kissed my neck, and this time it felt like a snake again.

"Yes you are her." He stated as he pulled back from my neck. I put my hand over the spot and stared at him. My mind could not come to grips with anything, my neck hurt, and yet I felt fine. I could not remember why I was afraid, but I felt like I should be. He felt wrong to me, but was familiar.

He held my cheek with his hand and smiled at me. It was not a pleasant smile and suddenly he did not feel as familiar.

"Your blood tastes of her. You see her life. You have her face. You are my wife. I will be back to claim you. However, I will leave you for a time, so that you may…." He paused and looked over me in a way that made me cringe. "Ripen to how I remember you."

He stood and before I could say anything he vanished. Simply vanished. I heard no voices, or whispers. I felt abandoned, then a bit frightened. I looked around and began to feel violated.

'He touched me without right or permission!' was my first thought as I came back to myself. I looked around and turned on the stone seat. He was nowhere to be seen. Then a thought occurred to me, 'People don't just vanish. I fail to see him because he wasn't real. I must have made him up so I would not have to think about all the other men in the room. If I focused on one, and the rest were no longer important.' It seemed a logical explanation for the illogical events I remembered.

"I have gone mad. The stress of the evening must have been getting to me and I just did not know." I stood to walk inside and nearly fainted. "Or maybe my corsets are just too tight." I said holding my sides, "I do feel a bit light headed."

The next thing I remembered was my Mother waving smelling salts under my nose.

"Your Father said to come inside, not to go play in the maze! Your debut ball and you still hide in here. If I hadn't had these Salts I would have had to go back and have someone carry you in. You would have looked very unladylike then."

Mother was walking beside me through the maze. I sat outside by myself. Father was standing me up. I heard Father telling the guests that I was tired and worn from the night's events. Then I was saying goodnight to everyone on the stairs.

Time was skipping, I was very lightheaded again, Mother kept her arm in mine to keep me standing. My eyes caught sight of Fredrick and he bowed his head at me as I was corralled up the stairs.

Father stayed down and the party continued. As we reached the landing I turned and looked down. Everyone had gone back to dancing. No one had seen a crazy man stalking me all night and no one had heard his voice.

'I must have been mad,' I thought. 'I just need to go rest' Mother was putting me to bed. When my corsets were off I felt better, but I was still feeling lightheaded.

"I will send someone to sit with you. I would stay myself but I must go back down and be with your Father. You rest, and don't get up unless it is necessary." She left the room.

I fell asleep.

I stop typing and stare at the screen. So many years ago, the memories are no longer as fresh. It is almost like I am writing about something that did not happen to me. Lifetimes have come and gone and my own memories are no longer vivid. All I could remember was pain, running, training. My whole life had always been about him.

"What else needs to be known?" I think about how to approach the rest of my mortal life. I look back over at the picture of Father,

Mother, and my former self. The picture was taken right before I was married. Should I write about the marriage, I thought.

I search through my memories to pick out the next place that was important to Adam's story. I start to write about a separate ball that was important before He cursed me.

Chapter 4
A Dance

Over the next year I was to start taking tea with my mother. I was to be socialized. I did not have any more strange voices in my ears. No strange fantasies came to me, and I never saw the man from my debut.

I started a new type of Etiquette training with my mother. I had already been taught how to sit, speak, laugh, and even eat.

Now, Mother was showing me how to be a wife, not just a girl in the chair. I was learning small points of business so I would be able to follow conversations. I learned what being a hostess was about, what my role was to be at dinners.

I was allowed to go to a few balls. I would sometimes see the young men from my ball. We would dance or smile at each other, but none of them asked for me, and I never wished for any of them. About half a year after mine, there was a debut ball for a young girl whose father worked with mine. We went that evening to show support for her father, and I was excited, it was my first evening out in awhile. Mother dressed us up. She was wearing a pale blue gown. She had not designed hers, as she had mine.

I was in green again, but this dress was more concealing. My debut dress hung in my room. This was not a night for me to shine, so I was to dress to be beautiful, but not overly so. A task I did not know could be accomplished, but it was.

My skirts were made of a satin material, with a lace pattern overlay that flowed from my waist on my right side, around the front of me to the floor on the left and slightly on the back.

My corset was still as tight. It was satin underneath the full lace cover. The satin stopped just above my chest, and flowed to the sides, over my arms. The whole top was covered by the lace that continued up to my neck. The lace collar was tight on my neck. It covered my shoulders and went down over the satin sleeves and past to my wrists. It was a sly way of showing my skin and shoulders, without being bare. The lacy top was the same pattern as the lace on the skirts so they flowed together, and looked like one solid dress. The satin was shining out from behind the lace so eyes would be drawn to me, but only when I was close.

Mother should have been a dressmaker. Once when I asked why she didn't make dresses, she said she didn't care about anyone else, that's why she only designed for me. She could only find ways to make me look better.

But the ball, please forgive side tracks my mind takes. These are memories I have not revisited for, in a long time. I may go off track it seems, but I feel if you understand me and my life, then you may understand Adam better. Well, let's see…

It was very similar to my ball. They also had a stairwell in the hall. It was straight against the wall, no landing, but with just a slight turn at the top onto the second floor.

We all stood in the hall, while her father stood a few steps up. He gave his thanks to us all for attending, and she stepped out onto the stairs from the second floor archway. She walked down and her father took her for her first dance.

I was able to watch from the side what it must have been like at my own ball. I could see all the people smiling, the young men nervously tapping their feet. One finally came forward and the dance started for everyone. I stayed on the sides of the dance floor. I didn't know what to do really.

I thought about going and sitting down when I spotted a man walking towards me. I turned to my mother and she smiled at me. I looked up to see the man who had come to a stop in front of me and was surprised.

"Fredrick!" I exclaimed, then blushed and lowered my voice, "How are you?"

"Pleased that you remembered me, Miss Tamson. I had thought that you might not remember one face out of the many you danced with at your own ball." He stopped and motioned to the dance floor with his right hand. "Would you like to dance again?"

His face was not as nervous as it was before, it was more firm, but not harsh. I missed seeing him nervous, but without it he was amazing. I gave him my right hand and we walked out a few steps and he started to dance. For some reason, maybe because eyes were not all on me, I felt like this dance was more intimate then at my ball.

I felt the graze of my skirts on his legs, the pressure of his hand upon my waist. I felt where his heart beat in his palm, the heat that radiated from him. We didn't talk during the first dance. We already knew each other so we could just dance. It gave me time to actually look at him.

Fredrick was a bit taller than me I noticed. My eyes were looking right at his chin if I looked forward. His dark brown hair was straight, except for the front, which was waved away from his face. It was very short in the back. However, you could not tell where the hair became short. His longer bangs flowed right into the trimmed hair in a way that made me stare. He had clear skin, a little darkened by being outside. I wondered what he did to be outside, but I didn't say anything.

He smiled at me, and then looked at our feet, then past our hands. I think he was just trying not to blush, but I took the chance to look at his profile and face. His nose was straight, tipped up at the end, but only slightly. You would miss it if you weren't looking, but it was there. I stared at his lips. They were not the thin lips I had grown up seeing on Father. He had a full lower lip and his top lip was almost shaped like a woman's, just more straight then curved. I was looking at his lips when they turned and smiled at me.

He didn't say anything but his smile was enough that I knew I had been caught looking. It was a polite smile but had undertones of laughter. I looked at my feet and then at our hands, as he had.

Everyone seemed to be dancing now. I could see on the side of the room, where some of the older women were conversing while the men were all talking business. We danced among the couples and looked around.

No others came and asked for my hand. I do not know if they were just waiting for the debutante, or if they thought Fredrick had already claimed me. I liked it though. I was allowed to just dance and have no worries about boring conversation and false smiles. There was no phantom voice or strange feelings this time. We danced to the end of the song without one word.

"My lady, you are a pleasure to dance with. Would you allow me another dance, or would you like to sit and rest your feet?" He smiled as we stood there waiting for the next song to pick up.

"I would much enjoy one more dance before we rest, Fredrick." A smile blossomed on his face as I said 'we rest' and he started a dance right away.

"Were you well after your ball Tamson? I know you were taken to your room. I had not a chance to thank you for the dances, or ask how you were." I looked down with a shy smile. It was wonderful that he worried about me, but how do I explain fainting from a phantom gentleman caller who waited for me in the maze?

"I was well. I simply became overwhelmed." I looked up at him and saw he really seemed interested, maybe even upset. "I went outside to get some fresh air and had a spell. Nothing very dangerous, I just needed to rest. Mother took me upstairs so I could rest and not make a scene at my own ball. It is all rather embarrassing, it was not very proper of me to go out on my own."

"There is nothing wrong with needing rest. I am just sorry that the evening was stressful to you. Hopefully this ball will not see you ill." He slowed our dance down and we turned in a slow circle. "I believe tonight I will be alright. I do not have to dance unless I wish to, so I can rest when I need to." I could see a slight smile brush his face. It made his jaw line stand out and he looked slightly older, but very handsome. I realized that my hand was placed on his arm and I could feel muscle through his jacket. I had never noticed before, but my stomach was all light. I was hardly noticing anyone else. While I was enjoying the dance he just led us around the room with a small grin.

I danced around wondering what had put the small grin on his face. When I realized that I had said 'I do not have to dance unless I wish to' and since I was happily dancing with him, it meant I wanted to. I had told him I liked him without even meaning to, without even realizing that I liked him. As soon as I realized that, I got shy and blushed. His grin turned into a smile, but he saved my feelings by leading us to the side.

"You look flushed, would you like to have a drink and rest a moment?"

We danced almost the entire night. He spoke of his schooling and how he was almost done and would be coming home to take over the family affairs. Near the end of the ball, we went over and talked to his mother for a while. He came and spoke business with Father for a bit, and I went to speak with Mother.

"You seem to be attached to his arm, little one. I have not seen you with dance with anyone else this night." She gave me a knowing glance but kept the smile off her face, even though I could hear it in her voice.

"Well, I talked to him briefly at my debut, and it was nice to have a longer discussion." I sipped on my glass and looked out to the dance floor. I didn't want her to see in my eyes that I had liked dancing with him.

"Really. A longer discussion." She nodded her head slightly as she thought. Her face was slightly tight as she tried harder not to giggle.

"When I would look at the two of you, I only saw smiles and hardly any talking at all." At this she did smile. Mother turned to me and her face was lit up.

"I hope that if he fancies you in return, that we will be able to arrange something. I wonder though. Do you believe he will be able to provide for you, if we were to go further on this? I would not want to talk to your Father about this young man if you were not happy with him." I was shocked at what my mother was saying, but realized that I was indeed of age, and was supposed to be married off. I thought about it for a moment and looked over at Fredrick.

"Mother I am not saying that I would like to marry Fredrick. I am not saying that I would not. I just have not thought about it. He makes me laugh and smile, this is true, but I have only seen him twice in my entire life." I looked down into my glass that Fredrick had brought me.

I wondered about what it would mean if I told my mother anything. Would they make me stop talking to him if I said I did not want to marry him? If I said I liked him, would they marry us tomorrow?

"He is still being schooled so I know he cannot provide for me as of now, but later I do not know. We may be happy together, but Mother, we have just met." I looked at her thinking that was final, we had just met, and we couldn't be married.

"Well, you go and finish off the night. I am feeling worn and will go see how long before we depart. I will take your father away from your young caller and you can think about what we have said." She turned and walked over to them. I sat down in one of the arm chairs near the window. I stared out into the evening. I could not believe my mother. I knew I was to be married off, but it had never occurred to me that I would be allowed a say in it. I thought they would just choose a caller and tell me I was going to be married. I was still pondering this when Fredrick walked over.

"I hope I am not interrupting anything." He smiled down at me. I looked at him and was slow in responding. It must have upset him because his smile faded and he sat near me. "Are you well?" He asked, with true concern.

"Oh yes. I am not going to have another spell. I was simply looking out at the evening. Are you done talking with Father?" I did not joke back as normal. I was looking at him and trying to see him as a husband instead of someone to talk to. Would he be a good provider, a good Father?

"Oh. I see. Well I hope your mother did not put you in a foul mood. Your smile seems to have faded."

"Oh we were talking about nothing. She just asked about us dancing." As soon as I said it I wished I had not.

"Really." His voice perked up a little. I could hear the teasing tone in it and should have been happy. If he could jest with me then he was not so worried, but I did not know what I would say. "And what did you say to her?"

"Oh nothing really. Just that you were a horrid dancer and I wished that she would rescue me." I smiled at him and we silently laughed. He looked out over the crowd and I looked at him.

He was handsome. I allowed myself to see it. Dark hair, with clear deep eyes. He wore his emotions on his face, which meant he was honest. His muscles and slight coloration meant that he did not mind working outside, but he was in school. He was going to be a business man, and with the land they owned he would be able to provide for me. I looked out on the dance floor, and before I knew what I was doing I blurted out.

"Mother was asking me if I thought you fancied me." I tried to say it nonchalantly. I feared what he would say, but was curious myself, and it came out a little too fast.

"Fancied you? Well, why would she think that?" He did not turn towards me but his eyes stopped moving and he sat still, but straightened up slightly. His voice did not have the joking tone as normal. With one sentence I had changed our conversation from a friendly chat into a tense discussion.

"I do not know. She said that we were smiling while we danced, and she noticed. I am sure she is suffering from delusions. I do not believe we were smiling more than anyone else. Were we?" I did not want to upset him. The conversation was too serious for me and I was trying to steer us away from it.

"I am sure no more than others. However, if you do not want her to be concerned, then we can dance with different guests. I am sure there are other gentlemen you would like to dance and converse with?" His tone was still businesslike, but he made the last a question. Something told me that, if I did not answer carefully, then he would be hurt, or leave. I realized I did not want either to happen.

"You better think again. If I have been smiling all night, then I see no reason to change my actions because Mother asks about them." I stared straight at him and he turned with a smile towards me.

"Well then, Miss Tamson would you like to dance, or would you like to accompany me outside for a breath of fresh air?"

"I would much enjoy a short walk outside." He walked over and held out his hand. For some reason though, I felt very feminine as I took it and he helped me stand. As he held open a smaller side door, I turned to make sure my dress was out of the door and saw Mother talking to Father. I secretly hoped they would not see us. After Mothers comments, I was not sure going outside alone was the best idea, but it sounded wonderful.

He closed the door. There were the main ones still open. He took my hand and we walked to the balcony. This house did not have a maze like mine, but a lovely rolling garden. There were high bushes hiding the large white brick wall around the grounds. Trees were spotted around the grounds, planted in the midst of flowers. Each had a small bench underneath for sitting.

In the middle of all of this, was an immense fountain that I would have loved playing in when I was a child. It had a sculpted figure on the top, of a mermaid combing her hair. There were ships carved into the stone at the bottom of the water reservoir.

"Miss Tamson, May I ask you a question?"

I looked at him and laughed. He turned his eyes toward me with a questioning glance and the moon lit up his face. I stopped laughing and just looked at him.

"You just did." To which he smiled back.

"Too true my lady, but would you be upset, if I asked a personal question?" I looked back out to the gardens. They were peaceful and would be wonderful during the day. I wished it was day now. Everything seemed so much more intimate at night, when the birds where quiet and even the air seemed to hold its breath.

"I cannot promise to not be upset. If it is personal then I do not know how I will react. However, you may ask. I promise that I will answer, if I am not upset. If I am upset, I will say that I am and you can think of another topic of conversation. Does that sound fair?" I looked back at him and his face had not changed. I could tell that he was thinking though. He was deciding how to word what he was thinking so I would not be upset. I began to worry. What could he want to ask that was so important?

"I do not wish to upset you. I will ask something else that I was also thinking. I am still at school as you know. I was wondering if you would not mind writing me when I go back." He looked away, hurried up, and spoke before I could say anything. "Small things about home. Possibly news about my mother if you see her of course. Nothing terribly important, just something to keep my days light while I am away?"

"I would be happy to Fredrick. Although I am not so sure what I could possibly write about that would matter. If I may though, that did not seem very personal. Now I am slightly curious as to what you were going to ask." I did not word it as a question, but I said it so he would understand I wanted to know. I glanced out over the gardens with a face uninterested, as to not seem so eager to know.

"Well Miss Tamson." He started, and then coughed slightly. He turned towards me. I saw him out of the corner of my eye, but kept looking out as if the topic was nothing to important. "I was thinking that your mother is a smart woman. She must see people for who they really are."

I turned my face to him slowly and it dawned on me that he did fancy me. I was a little surprised, a little happy, but a little scared. Was he only being nice to me because he enjoyed my face? Was I just a business venture to the one man who had made me smile all evening? I tried to keep my face neutral as I looked up at him.

"Am I to assume, if you think Mother can see the real person inside, that she might be correctly seeing interest on the dance floor?" I asked slightly amused. I tried to make a joke, but the question was very serious.

He cleared his throat ever so slightly and looked out to the gardens. He seemed taller while he was thinking. I looked up at him and realized that if he did fancy me, and all went orderly, I may be spending the rest of my life with him. A moment ago, we were just friends a few years apart in age. Now it seemed like I was a child looking at a man, but this man did not scare me in any way. I felt that I could be happy if we were married, and would always wonder, if we were not.

"Miss Tamson, please know that it was not my intention to bring you out here to discuss such things, I truly do enjoy talking to you. It was however, my intention to come to this ball, in hopes of seeing you again." He paused for a moment, I could see thoughts roll past his eyes, but he did not move. I stayed quiet in case he had more to reveal, I did not want to misunderstand his intentions due to me interrupting.

"I had a wonderful time dancing and being with you, at your own ball. Though I did not know for sure if you had enjoyed my company, or if you were simply being a gracious hostess. I knew your father would be invited this evening, and came in hopes that you would be here. I wanted to see if you would enjoy my company, when you weren't being forced to dance with every gentleman that asked." He stopped just long enough to take a breath.

At first it sounded like he was gathering his strength, but it ended sounding like a sigh.

"I would like to talk to your father about you, because I do enjoy spending time with you, and I find you very beautiful. Your mother was right to see how I smiled, I do fancy you. However." and he breathed deep again, "I could not imagine speaking to your father without knowing if you could ever be happy with me. I know you have only seen me twice, but I already feel like I could be happy with you by my side. I wanted to see if there was the possibility of that happening. I did not want to bring it up at the present moment, but since it has been brought up already, I want to just ask."

He finally looked fully at me and seemed to shrink down and become softer. He held a hand out, touched mine, curled his fingers around mine and lifted them between us. I faced him and looked up, not knowing how to react to the question that Mother had helped bring early.... Or had I? If I had not been curious, I would not have brought it up and then I could have thought longer.

"Tamson, I feel like I could grow to love you, I already love hearing your laugh and seeing your smile. I do not ask anything permanent of you now. I am asking you just to look in your heart, and let me know if it is just friendship that brings our smiles, or if it could one day be more. I ask much from you, but I promise I will not move any further, except to be your friend, if your answer is no. Should you prefer someone else, that is your heart. I would like to stay friends, but I would know to put my attention elsewhere. I know your father can still say no, and make no arrangements with me, but I would like to know your heart, not his. So." He sighed once more. "I put the question to you. If I spoke to your father, and he arranged it, could you find it in your heart to be happy with me, or would you be left wanting in a life with me?" He stared at me, but put no push, he simply waited.

Although I knew what he had been thinking, I had not thought he would ask me in this manner. I was told that Father might get some talks right away. I was even warned that I might not even see the young man before Father introduced us. Here I was, being given a chance to consider my own thoughts and feelings. Before Father even knew, and would ever know if I said 'No'. I looked down at our hands and looked inside myself. I smiled a little and looked up.

"I had never thought to be asked my opinion. I thought that maybe it would have been dealt with like a business deal. That alone makes me happy if nothing else could. I thank you for thinking about me." I smiled and stared up at him, His face was cautious. I had said nothing about my heart, just showed appreciation for his manners.

"While I cannot promise that I will always be happy, I am not unwilling to try."

At this he squeezed my hands and smiled bigger then I had ever seen him smile before and I giggled.

He laughed and I looked down to hide my amusement. I thought that when I was going to be married, I would be afraid. However, I was almost anxious now. I knew my future, possibly. If Father allowed it, then I would be married, but to someone who I chose.

He reached up with one hand and touched my chin. I looked up at him, thinking he was going to say something else. However he just leaned in smiling and laid a kiss upon my lips. Barely a touch. He brushed his lips lightly across mine, my smile froze. I stood as if I was made of the same stone as the statue in the garden. I closed my eyes and I breathed in the night. Everything was crisp and wonderful. When I opened my eyes, he was just watching me. Waiting for me to open my eyes again just so he could see them.

"Lets us go back inside. I can speak to your father tonight, or we can keep it for us. I will call upon him tomorrow if you would prefer it." Fredrick seemed suddenly a man who was grown and stronger. I looked up at him and thought, 'I could truly be happy.' I put my hand on his elbow and started to walk slowly to the open doors.

"No you may go in and speak with Father so he knows your intentions. It would not be pleasing to learn that another man inquired of me for business, when I have a man who thinks to ask if I could be happy. I will speak with Mother and let her know that I fancy you as well. This way she can tell Father to agree." I smiled my mischievous smile to my toes waiting for his response. He pulled my hand slightly and I looked back with an innocent look.

"So 'she can tell Father', am I to look forward to being told what to do?" he asked.

"Most assuredly you may." I said with a smile and I walked inside pulling him up to me as we both laughed.

We went in and walked towards my parents. I turned to walk to Mother as he smiled, squeezed my hand before letting go and walked to Father. When I told her of his proposal, she hugged me and smiled.

"I knew he fancied you, but I did expect a bit longer before we had any true callers. Well, I hope you will both be happy with your choice."

The next day my father spoke with him formally. We were scheduled to be married when Fredrick returned from his last year at school. I would be his wife by the end of the year, and my mother started planning our wedding.

Though Adam was nowhere to be seen at that ball, I felt that you should see that I was normal at one point. That I had a life all of my own, and was happy. For Adam did come back into my life, and ruined it all.

"I guess the proper place to pick up would be after the wedding." I say to myself as I stretch my arms.

Writing about the ball and Fredrick had makes me smile. I do have happy memories still. I thought all that was left was pain and suffering but as I wrote, I was giggling with the memories of his shyness. I had closed my eyes when I was writing about our first kiss. Looking back I realize I had truly loved him and part of me still does.

Now I have to write about our marriage and when Adam came back into my life. I do not want to ruin the memories that have me smiling, but I am not writing to remember. I am writing to inform, my memories are just a lesson.

I take a deep breath, and begin writing about the ruin of my life. I skip the wedding day, my dress and the ceremonies are unimportant to the reason for my writing. What is important, though, is what happened after we were married.

Chapter 5
A Honeymoon?

I will jump to after our wedding. I was so excited the days leading up to the wedding. So nervous was I that whole day, waiting for that moment when I became a wife. So happy to say my vows. We laughed and smiled throughout the dinner.

After dinner I became scared and nervous in a different manner. Adam had visited me again, but he had wiped it from my memories. What I am writing took place a few nights after we were married.

I was uncomfortable in his bed chambers, so he had arranged for my own room. This is the first conversation I believe we had, that fits in with what you need to know.

"Don't come any closer, please." I could not think of anything else to say. This was my husband and I was still afraid to have him near me. Something was wrong with me.

I had felt off ever since we had been married. Although I did not know why, it reminded me of my debut ball. When I was supposed to be having the time of my life but something bothered me throughout the whole thing. I had imagined a man to take me out of the reality. The stress of the evening overwhelmed me and I felt out of control. I had since forgotten most of my ball, except a few moments with Fredrick, my Father, and a fogging memory of being in the maze.

That's what our marriage was like. I knew at the time I wanted to be married, I was not afraid. Now, however, I could not think of why I would have agreed. I remember spending days imagining our life together, but I could no longer see the images. I just felt uncomfortable and worried all the time. I just felt out of control and that nothing would go as I wanted. All the good feelings I had for Fredrick were still there, just hidden behind a fog and I could not reach them. I knew I had felt for him, but could not remember why.

Sometimes I would see the maze in my dreams, when my mind is trying so hard to remember. In the dreams the maze was mixed with a home and the place haunted me. It pulled on my heart even when I was awake, though I could not remember it. It haunted me and stopped me from enjoying life like others could. They were not like me, living in a dream world they could not escape.

"Why should I not come near my own wife?" Fredrick asked me, bringing me back to reality from my thoughts. I was spending more time worried about my mind then I was living.

"I have never caused you harm, never threatened you." He sat down in a lounge chair near my door. His voice had grown tired, worried and hurt in just the few days I had been his. He put his hands down in his lap and looked down as he spoke to me. I felt bad knowing it was my fault, I wanted to comfort him, but I could not let myself go near.

"I asked for your hand because I thought you had some feeling for me. When I first asked, you seemed happy to marry. The past year you seemed like it could not happen soon enough. I did not know if you truly loved me, but I thought that if you did not already, you may learn to love me. I try my hardest to make you smile again, but you pull away more each day. On our wedding day you seemed so happy, but after that you seemed to withdraw. I am saddened to see you unhappy, Tamson. I now ask only that you try to see the devotion I show you, the love I offer. I hope you will give us a chance."

My heart felt heavy. I was bringing tears to a once happy home. I felt that I could not be happy there, but I knew that I had wanted to be here. I had wanted to marry him, I was happy on our wedding day. I could not understand why I felt so uneasy here now.

He turned just his face towards me and looked at me with unshed tears in his eyes. "I know you could learn to live with me and the life I provide, if only you would open up to me. I thought we would be happy together. You seemed happy before, but I see now you are not. Maybe it is shock, maybe I am not what you thought I was." He paused and I could tell he blamed himself for my new attitude. It was wrong, it wasn't him, but my mind kept saying it was. How did I let him know it was alright and it wasn't him, when I couldn't say that it wasn't?

"Just know that this is your home as well now. You should not feel uncomfortable in your own home. You should not fear to be close to me. Please just tell me why you feel you must pull away from me, and I will try to help you. I am the man who provides for you now, who cares for you, protects you. I cannot do so if you hide what bothers you."

He stared at me with such longing that I wanted to cry for him. I had caused him this aching. I did not deserve such loyalty.

"My husband, I do not fear you, and nothing threatens me that you need to protect me from. I just have not been feeling well." I looked up at him and tried to give a brave face that would show him no worry, "Adjusting to this new life has been hard on my heart, although you have made the time easier for me. I am grateful for your devotion and do not mean to seem without feelings toward you. I am sure it is just female emotions."

He did not seem comforted at all. I realized I sounded very stiff and not at all like I was trying to enjoy my new life. I looked at him and forced and apologetic smile.

"I asked that you do not come near me because I fear that I am getting ill. I would like nothing more than to be held and made better, but I do not want you to also fall ill." I tried to give my most sincere face.

Despite the odd feeling of danger and unease I felt, I truly longed to be held by Fredrick, and make him smile as I had before. It would have been so nice to be held and talked to, but I knew that within minutes I would feel the dread again.

It was not towards me, but I would feel that my husband was in trouble. I kept away from him because I was afraid that I would hurt him. I was afraid that, the dread I felt was, the part of me that dreamt odd dreams, would hurt him for being in front of that dream. I did not make sense to myself, so how could I allow him to get close.

I was so confused. I did not know if I was mentally sane so I was afraid to ask anyone if this was normal for new brides. I was happy to be married; now I was unhappy all the time. I wanted to be held and remembered loving him, but could not find the emotions now. I longed to hold him or be held, but when I got over the nervousness and touched him I felt like he was in trouble, that I was doing wrong. If these odd thoughts really were from me, was I mad? Would I hurt him without knowing?

The worry and stress really was making me feel ill. I felt that at least I was not completely lying when I told him I was unwell.

"I am sure some rest will cure me of my unease. I did not mean to sound so short with you, Fredrick. I just do not wish to bring illness to you as well." It was the closest to the truth that I could tell him. If I was mad, I did not want to make anyone else insane as well.

"My dear sweet Tamson. You are unwell, and still think of my well-being. I had not realized that our wedding day had caused you undue stress and illness. Of course after having a spell at your debut I knew big events would have a toll on you. I forgot completely in my own happiness and I am sorry I was not more observant to you. However I now know you do think of me, and for that I am grateful. Even if I had to find out through a misunderstanding that hurt for a short time, it warms my heart now. I shall let you rest." He stood and straightened his shirt. Trying to erase the emotions from his face before he would go out into the house where he was supposed to be the 'Man'.

"I am sorry for my display of unwarranted emotions. I do not want to stress you further. I shall send up a kitchen maid with some tea. Maybe bring up a nice broth to warm your throat?" He stared at me with such love in his eyes, true worry over my health, and happiness that he might be able to help me. I wondered how long he had been waiting for me to show him some affection, I smiled with genuine happiness. He looked as happily nervous as when I first met him.

"That sounds wonderful, MY husband. Thank you so much." I made sure to use words that would make him happy and he smiled. I felt happy that I brought it to his face, but wished the words hadn't made me feel sick. I wondered why I could not be happy with him, when moments like this I felt like I could be, like I should be when he smiled at me.

"I am glad you thought of such, I might have stayed up here and gotten worse for hunger, were you not thinking of me. A small bowl of vegetable broth sounds perfect, and a warm cup of tea would help me sleep. Maybe I will rise tomorrow feeling rested and well again."

I really would have stayed up in my room getting hungry, but not for those reasons. I just wouldn't have wanted to leave the room after I had told him I was feeling ill. Although I could have called someone from the kitchen for something to eat, it would have been possible that Fredrick would have thought I was just avoiding him. That would have made it harder for me. He really did care for me, and it made me sad that I could not return his emotions without bringing him harm, or myself confusion.

"I will have them bring it up at once. I will have someone check on you to see if you need anything else." He gave a small bow of his head, and a small smile.

I realized that I rarely saw his smile any more, and I missed it. "I will retire as well, Good night Tamson. I hope tomorrow sees you a better day." I smiled at him and his smile grew with mine. He turned and looked back at me as he left the room. I could almost see him sigh with relief. I had shown him something he had been waiting for since we married.

He shut the door slowly and latched it quietly as to not hurt my head if it was also hurting. He thought only of my happiness and well being, and I thought only of my own worries. It seemed he cared more for me then I did myself. I wanted to love him in return, but was afraid to do so.

I sat down in the arm chair by my window and stared out into the evening. Night brought peace and rest, but I always felt like something was stalking me. I hated the feeling, but was oddly soothed by the night. I just looked out and breathed in the night air, as I pondered my odd feelings.

There was a small knock on the door, I turned my head towards the room and told them they could enter before looking back out the window. I felt like a rich snobby woman who thought too much of herself. Sitting by the window being waited on instead of being a wife, but the night calmed me and I could not tell anyone why I was so worried.

"Evening." I turned to see who it was, and was staring at a woman so motherly I at once liked her. "Oh Miss. You should not sit so close to the window if you are not feeling well. I know a thing or two about illness if I do say so myself. Raised three children of my own while I've worked here, and I helped with the house young ones. Sitting next to the night chill will bring you further restless nights."

She set down a tray on the small table near the fireplace and hurried over to bring me a housecoat. She helped me into it and walked me over to the chaise lounge by the fire place. She looked to be in her late 40's, though time had aged her through work, happiness shown in her face. She worried over me like I was a child who had just fallen in the snow with no jacket.

"How long have you worked here miss…?"

"You may call me Miss Ivy, though I hope in time you will call me

Millie. It's a name my children gave me and I like it when the member of this household feels close enough to me to use it. I am sorry I was not here when you joined this family and came to live with Master Fredrick. My oldest, Edward, has just blessed me with a grandchild and I was given a month to go and see the blessed thing. Still, I so wish I had been here to make you feel at home. I have been here for so long this feels my family as well." She smiled down at me and then went to rouse the fire to bring more warmth to the room.

When she was finished she came to look at me and had an odd but knowing look upon her face.

"Madam do you wish for me to go, or would you like some company? I can stay and take away your tray, or you can just ring for me when you are finished." I knew it was her way of telling me she'd sit with me. I thought about it, I felt like I had nothing much to say. Yet I also felt that I had spent too much time alone tonight. Too much time inside my own thoughts with nothing much to think about.

"First Miss Ivy, please do not call me Madam. I do not feel like I deserve it as I am still very much a child. You may call my Tamson, or Miss Tamson, if you need some sort of formality. Secondly, I should like very much for you to sit with me. I would also like to feel like this is my family and spending time with you would help me feel warmer." She smiled and sat down in a chair near me. Though she did not look relaxed, I could see she was. She just had a straight back and was fulfilled with her life.

"May I ask how you came to work here? I should like small conversation instead of quiet while I try to eat health back into me." I smiled at her hoping to get the response I was looking for. I needed someone I could jest with or I would never feel at home.

"I would not mind telling you about my life. Firstly, however, I know you come from a good family and would have had a good nurse. There is no doubt in my mind that neither your nurse, nor parents, would have let you believe that simple broth will bring you anything but warmth." She gave me a teasing reprimanding face and smiled before she went on. "You need rest, so no chatter about eating health."

We smiled at each other. I had someone who understood my odd humor. She may not like it or joke back at me, but she understood I was not serious and would amuse me. I could live with that.

"Before I go on with my story, I should ask you something. Why do you want to know about me?" She asked me. I thought about it and answered honestly.

"Miss Ivy, I am not comfortable here yet. I did not even know you worked here, and in my family's house, I knew all our help. I knew their lives, and played with their children. I would like to know about the people in this house as well. Maybe not knowing everyone is part of why I feel down." I paused and sipped my tea and looked at her. "Also, I should like a nice long story that has nothing to do with me to take my mind off my worries."

"Well that I can do." She laughed. "I can most assuredly spin long tales. I would be happy to tell you about my life if it helps you even through one night. If you feel more at home knowing me, then who am I to leave you wanting." She looked into the fire and smiled as she sighed. She glanced at me and started her story.

"I came to work for this family when I was not much older then you. My mother had worked here in her day, we were not too proud to work for our living. Not that I think you have to work hard to be a good person. I just find that bringing help into someone's life brings more people into your heart and makes you feel more like you belong, no matter where you call home.

My grandfather was not by any means rich or thought too highly of. He was well off though, as he owned the best bakery in town. He had done all the baking and selling, and my grandmother kept house and the children. When my grandmother died his heart seemed to shut down.

Though he still loved my mother and uncle, he could find no passion. His loss of emotion included his love of baking. Without my grandmother Eve, the bakery seemed empty to him. He started to lose customers and one day decided to just close the shop." She shifted her weight and I did not know if it was the memories or the chair that made her uncomfortable, but she just settled back and went on.

"They had a good amount of money from selling the bakery building, but it left them with no income. My mother had been learning small baking tips from Grandmother, but her real passion was in sewing.

She became an assistant for a boutique that made one of a kind clothes for well to do families. All the gowns were handmade and anyone who worked on the sold gown received payment. So my mother began working on any gown she could, so people would know her and ask for her." Miss Ivy turned to me as she continued the story.

"Now one of the regular customers there was Master Fredrick's own grandmother. She was a sharp woman who noticed every little detail and started to recognize my mothers work and liked it. She told the shop owner that she wanted my mother to assist on all her gowns because they always came out perfect. After awhile of being a regular customer she became a little fond of Mother and would talk friendly to her while at the shop.

One day she noticed that my mother was looking thinner and sadder than normal. After a small discussion during a fitting, she discovered that my family's money situation was not so well and Mother was worried that they would not be able to bring themselves out of it this time. Later that week Mother was given a letter addressed to my grandfather. He read it and the next day came to this very house.

"When he returned to his house, he told my mother and uncle he had been offered a position as the family's new cook. If he did not want the position, they requested that he come and be a baker for special occasions, when they called on him.

He wanted the opinions of my mother and uncle because if he accepted, they would all be moved to a servant's house on the family grounds. They would be treated as friends not servants, because the move was only to ensure that he would be close if his services were required. My mother and uncle were both excited. By the end of the month my family had their own house on the grounds and money troubles were over." She paused and took a breath looking in the fire. She poked a few logs closer together and stared at my broth sitting there.

"Even if you are this interested in my story, you do need to eat before that gets cold."

She finished her story too quickly, skipping details and helped me get ready for bed before leaving. Whether it was uncomfortable for her, or she just wanted me to rest, I did not know. She did not talk much about her own parents much; just that she grew up in this house. We slowly became friends over time.

After that I did start to feel more at home. I started to learn more about the servants, and each had good things to say about the family.

The house started to feel like home, yet I still was uncomfortable with Fredrick. I did not understand why, but I still felt like something would happen if I became happy here

I would walk around the house, eat and talk to everyone while he was away on business. When he would go out to check the fields I would go with him. He felt like he was spending time with me and I could look out the window. We still did not sleep in the same room.

I had told him I got better, but in my state of mind I was still nervous about wifely duties. He understood and told me that as long as I was happy in his home, he could wait for me to be comfortable.

He was a great husband. I could see that in the way he held my hand, the love in his eyes, the complete understanding. I just could not bring myself to feel it back. I became a queen of acting and deceptive speaking. I remembered loving him before. I just could not find it inside me anymore.

I would have dreams at night of the whole house walking in the fields. I would see a cottage in the distance and start walking, squinting trying to see it. Someone held me back and it was always Fredrick. I hated him for keeping me from that cottage and would fight him. I would try and break free, run across the grass. Anytime I was free someone else from the house would catch me. I would wake feeling trapped and resentful of this house.

Other nights I dreamt of our dances and I felt happy. But when it felt like that happiness was finally real, a shadow started to form in the corners of the dream. The dance would turn to Fredrick just holding me against my will and I would wake scared.

With the sun rising I would feel better and could enjoy the day. However, I could never find my feelings for Fredrick during the day, only in dreams that ended in me crying.

I stop typing and sit staring at the computer. I feel the sun approaching my city. He was resting for the day, his energy was dim. He was east of me, but closer then yesterday. He was closing in on me and I would have to hurry.

Soon I would be fighting for my life. I save the words I've written. I had also bought a small device I can plug into the computer and it would save files. I save my story on that as well. The salesman had told me that in case my computer was broken or unavailable, I could still write in the same files using this. I was going to send the device to the Witch as soon as I finish writing. With it I was going to send instructions that she read the files only if she felt my death.

I finish saving the files and head to the bedroom thinking about the Witch. My life had been so happy. I had been a nervous new wife, but I have learned most new brides are. Later I had even found happiness.

Why couldn't He have left me alone? Why couldn't I have stayed happy? Why couldn't I have been a mother and grown old with my husband?

I wouldn't be here today, but I also wouldn't be feeding off others and hiding and fighting for my life.

I know that tomorrow night I have to write the end. It was a beginning, but it always feels like an end when I remember.

I lie down and pull my covers up. I send a small prayer to the heavens that he would not find my city for a few more nights. I want time to finish my lesson.

I could not fail, but if I did. It would all start again. He would find me again. I could not have that, he would have to be killed, or he would just wait for me again. Growing more twisted each year, growing more and more evil until he found me and I would have to endure this all again.

I fall into a troubled sleep and am not relaxed as I wake. I can feel the night coming and so I sit and waited. I didn't spend much energy last night so I woke before sunset. I wait for the sun to leave the sky and go to the bathroom to wash up.

It was too much work to cover up all the windows in each house or apartment I get. Bedroom windows are easy and I explain that away because I work during the night. So it's understandable to have a dark bedroom during daylight. If I went through each of my homes and covered up all the windows, it would be more noticeable and harder to hide from Adam. He was in every aspect of my life, even when I had left Him behind.

After a quick wash up and I put my hair up, and get dressed. Luckily it was late in the year and no one would notice me bundled up. On with a sweater and a scarf. Tonight I twist up my hair, grab a short hair brown wig and a woolen hat to put on. It wouldn't hide me from Adam if he saw me, but the less red heads seen around here might hold him off one night.

Tonight I want to be further away from my apartment when I feed. Too many injuries in one area and it will draw attention. Local authorities can almost be as big a pain as He is.

I human speed race walk a few blocks and catch a cab to a bad part of town. I normally lived in less than respectable areas, but never in the really bad areas. I needed the less friendly neighbors, but I could not stand so much distasteful happenings around me. It always reminds me of Him.

Once there, I pay the cabby and start walking. Pretty soon I saw my victims. I sigh try to ignore that lump in my throat. As always I remind myself that I have to do this or I'll die. If I want to make anything good of this life I have to survive. So I wait for them to catch up to me.

They were leaving a bar and are very drunk. I lean up against the corner of a bar next to an alley. I undid my scarf and played with the ends of it.

They got closer and saw me. I hear their hearts beat faster and their scents changed. I hate sensing the physical changes in humans when they got excited about me, and all I need was them as food. It always makes me feel evil and dirty and made them too real for me. I smile at them and they start walking again.

I decide right there I don't want to play games, I always feel worse when I did that. I sense no one else was around so as I caught their eyes, I capture their minds and walk them to the end of the alley. I have the taller one sit down and wait.

I could feed off one person tonight, but Adam was close so I want more energy just in case. Besides, two victims, while sad, means I can drink less from each and still get more power. Better all around, if I have to be evil, I try to be a good evil.

I begin to drink from the first man. I drink just a little. I normally don't think much about them as I drink, with blood can come knowledge.

If you think about them, you learn about them. Only this time as I taste him, I taste his bad heart. I can't take much from him because it would hurt him later. He drank alcohol because he couldn't stand his bodies weakness.

I have to pull away because his thoughts and dreams and fears started to flow. I clean his wound and put a bandage on his neck. He would remember cutting his neck while shaving before a night out.

I sit him down and reached for his friend. I cut his neck slightly and lean in to feed. I make the mistake of thinking about his friend's heart and pull back a second. I have to clear my head. While I start to feed I think of a chant monks had taught me that would stop any thought from entering ones head. I stop long enough to check how much blood I have taken.

As soon as I stop the chant in my mind, a single thought enters my mind.

If his friend drinks because he can't stand his body, why did this man drink?

His blood flowed with the truth that he was a great man. A husband and father. He came out with his friend to drink because he doesn't know how else to support him. He is in perfect condition and his life is good, while his best friend seems to have everything go wrong with him.

Before I can stop myself, I wonder how his friend's life was so bad. I am flooded with memories of high school friends, boys spending nights in tree houses. Abusive parents, bad grades, bullies at school, no money.

Mark.

His name was Mark. He went to college to get away from it all. They stayed friends through everything and now Mark was a lonely man, with a weak body, who never tried for a family because of his parents. His only problem, mentally and physically, was his parents never took care of him. Derek was his friend through everything and now he had a family and children and a perfect life.

Derek. I was eating from Derek.

I stop and almost throw up the blood I was drinking. I had gotten too much from him. Not too much blood, but too much life. I knew him now and I can't feed from someone who isn't bad in some way. His only vice was he drank, but he did so to help his friend. They were both good people who cared for others. I sat down beside them, and cried.

I cannot stand violence, and I have just abused a man who grew up with it.

I had fed from Derek, and he was a good man. Their blood, even with the alcohol in it, will give me more power and energy than others. Tainted blood, tainted by evil, bad deeds, or even drugs, was less powerful. It tasted worse, and never really filled the hunger. Even though it kept me weaker, I always drank it. I could not bring myself to hurt an innocent.

He had told me many times, that if we only drank from innocents, we would be all powerful. They have not tainted themselves and therefore have more pure blood, more powerful blood. That blood will be sweet and would curb the hunger. The more we drank the more power we would have.

Since I broke away from Him, I have never drunk from innocents. Never. I know that their blood did give us more power, but only because their blood nourished us better.

We never would have become all powerful, even drinking from innocents only. It does cause me to wonder if he truly believed it though. The thoughts of his, which lead to this curse, may have grown into the belief that he could become all powerful. I may never know.

However, I tried so hard to be nothing like Him, I had almost killed myself. My first years away from him I tried drinking from animals, from murderers, from people drugged out. I found out the hard way that blood that is too tainted is almost like not feeding at all. It does not fill the hunger, but it also does not nourish.

So I always drink from someone with small bad deeds, humans with light drugs in the blood. I always feel hungry, but at least I get nourished.

Tonight though, I will feel more powerful then I have in a long time, because they were good people. Derek would not even have talked to me if I had not captured his mind. He has always been faithful to his wife, even in his thoughts. Mark would have looked at me, but not tried anything. The alcohol was the only thing they did wrong, and that, at least for Derek, was for his friend. I had been in so much of a hurry I didn't really look at them. I just saw two drunken guys and used them.

Innocents have pure blood, sweet, powerful. Derek and Mark were the most innocent people I had drank from in over 100 years. I cry for them. I cry for me. Then I cry as I run away. I run home, not caring if He felt my energy. He was far enough away it would take two nights at least to get here.

I go to my room and tear off the hat and wig and scarf and stare at my reflection. I can see the difference. My skin has a more lifelike color to it. My hair shined. My eyes are clear, even through the slightly red tears. I'm even flushed.

"I have to kill Him." I say aloud to my reflection. "He did this. To me. To everyone. I have to finish this."

I walk to the computer, turn it on, and wait for it to load everything up. I stare down at my fingers. My nails are clearer, they even look longer. I can hear everything in the apartments building. I am indeed more powerful tonight then I have been in a long time.

I calm myself down, put Derek and Mark out of my mind. I open my eyes and I am still looking down at my fingers. It reminded me of what I was writing and the first time he came to change me. The file was loaded and it is time to write.

Chapter 6
Happy Days

The next time in my life that is relevant to Him and His evil, would be about six months later. I had lived in the house for half a year and only been with my husband, as a wife, once.

Our wedding night was the only time we had been together. For six months I had slept in my own chambers, made friends with everyone in the house, but still kept my husband at a distance.

One night however, I had an odd dream. While I was sleeping, I dreamt of myself sleeping. The dream was full of oppressiveness and I wanted to wake up but I couldn't.

In this dream I felt like a man was in my room. He was staring at me, and I felt the danger, but could not move. Inside my head I screamed to wake up but nothing happened.

This man came over and stood beside me and whispered something about wanting me too much. That he had to leave before he did the change too early.

I heard the words but did not understand them. I heard him say that I was beautiful, but not quite ready. So he was leaving until I was perfect. Then he walked out of the room.

When I woke I remembered a scary dream, but the images faded fast. I remembered them later and that is how I can tell you the dream. However, that morning, I woke and it faded.

As it faded though, so did most of my worries. I knew that when I got close to Fredrick I would be uncomfortable, but I did not know why. Even as I thought that, the feeling left. I felt like I could do anything.

I went down for breakfast. He was already seated at the table in the kitchen, reading a book. The small table in the kitchen that was meant to hold food, before it was served in the dining room, but that was where he ate. Not to avoid me, as I always did to him, but because it was more comfortable. He was friends with his help, and everyone in the house, except me. I always pushed him away, but I could not remember why. I started to leave as usual, but stopped.

Even though I was still in my nightgown with just a housecoat on, I did not feel a need to hide. He had not heard or seen me so I could easily slip back upstairs, but I felt I shouldn't have to.

I walked in and went to sit down, across the table, but at least I didn't leave.

"Good Morning Fredrick, Did you sleep well?" I tried to sound normal, but I felt so light that I was smiling. I couldn't remember the last time I smiled when I wasn't with Millie.

"Tamson. Yes, I slept well. Thank you. I take it you are rested?" He had learned caution around me. I am sure that Millie kept him informed about me, but I had not spoken much to him because I had felt overwhelmed. Today was a different day in many ways, I felt absolutely at ease and comfortable. It was surprising and very welcome.

"Believe it or not, I slept terribly. I had a dream I could not wake from that frightened me. However, when I woke, that dream faded. As the dream faded I felt better than I have in ages. It is almost as if I dreamed away my troubles." I smiled at him as I picked up a croissant.

Millie's grandfather had died a long time ago, but had he taught his recipes to the next baker, and they became household recipes. The croissants were always fresh and delicious.

He laughed lightly which made me smile more. That made me think. I swallowed the bread and looked at him. He stopped laughing and just looked back at me. He looked happy, but cautious. I hated to see that caution in his eyes.

I stood up and walked over to his side of the table. I sat down beside him and noticed his quick glance at me before he looked back down at his book as if my moving meant nothing. I wondered how many times he's been careful not to notice me for fear of scaring me.

I instantly felt love for him again. He truly cared for me and had gone through six months of disappointment. He has been married and left his wife alone to keep her happy. I was undeserving of such devotion.

I reached over and touched his hand, I felt him go suddenly still. It seemed even his heart was waiting. I looked at his hand as I spoke.

"Fredrick, I know I have made life hard for you. I hope that you have not lost any of your feelings for me during this time. Today I feel like a new person and I want you to know that I do feel for you. I also want to ask that you do not give up on me. If tomorrow I am not feeling right again, I want you to hold onto hope, because I do want to make our life together work." I looked up at his face and smiled. "I really do want it to work. I want to smile and jest with you again. I want to wake up and know that I make your face light up."

I leaned over and held him to me, with both arms. He leaned his head on my shoulder and I felt the breath he'd been holding leave him.

"I'm sorry I've taken this long to tell you that I care. I am hoping that whatever was bothering me has gone forever, but if I should feel off again, please do not give up on me."

He moved away so that he could look in my eyes.

"Tamson I would never give up on you. I am so happy that you came to me on your own, and I will always make life the way you want it. Even if tomorrow you do not wish to be near me, I will try to make you happy. Let us just hope that does not happen" He smiled at me and I laughed.

Really laughed.

He laughed with me and hugged me tightly. He went to let go of me so I could be free to do as I wanted. He stood up from the table and was turning to walk off.

I reached up and pulled him in for a quick hug, leaned up and laid a kiss on his cheek. He was so shocked he simply stood there. I giggled knowing that I could stop him with something so simple.

"I think I love you." I said to him as I smiled up at him. I saw the worry of the past six months actually lift off his shoulders as he leaned in and gathered me in his arms. Fredrick kissed me so deeply that I almost felt like laughing, but it was too serious a kiss to giggle. I wrapped my arms around his shoulders and let myself go. He held me tightly but it did not feel oppressive. I enjoyed the feeling as he held me up slightly so I wouldn't have to be on tip toe. He stopped kissing me, placed his head on mine and kissed my nose. He took a breath and let me go slowly.

"Sorry Tamson. I did not mean to not ask, but I've just waited a long time to hear those words from you." He looked down at me with an almost scared look. He thought I was going to run.

"I just could not hold back. If I only got to kiss you this once, I wanted it to be worth my time." He smiled down at me and it was a true smile. He was happy, and teasing me a little.

"I guess I am glad that I am worth your while then." I joked back at him and we laughed lightly as he wrapped his arms around my shoulders.

Just like that, our lives were changed. He was not afraid to talk to me. I was not afraid to be close to him. I felt at home and could not remember why I had felt oppressed in the first place.

A week of sleeping in the room by myself and I felt I had been there long enough. I spoke to him one evening after dinner. We were in the sitting room. He didn't smoke a pipe like Father but he did enjoy a glass of port, which I had started drinking just a few days before, when I started spending my evenings with him.

I turned to him and put my glass to my lips. I took a small sip and decided to just say it.

"Fredrick." He looked up at me and smiled, he was no longer cautious with me. It had been a week and we had been having a wonderful time being friends again. It's surprising how fast things can change, better or worse. "I was thinking. I don't know why it has taken this long, but I feel." I paused trying to word it right.

"I'm tired of being happy with you, but not waking up beside you. I don't want to ruin this past week, but I feel I want to try. I want to know what it's like to fall asleep beside you and wake with you." I purposely left out anything physical, because I was not sure yet if I was ready for it. I did know that I was tired of being by myself at night. I looked back down into my glass and sipped the port. When all else fails, act like nothing matters to you.

"Well, if you want to try, I guess we could leave all your things in your room. That way if you feel odd, you can go and sleep there. We can even sneak you to my room if you don't want Millie finding out." I laughed and threw a pillow at him.

Just like that I was going to sleep in his room that night. I did not feel apprehensive, in fact, I was a little excited. Since he had not mentioned anything physical, I was thinking about it. He had joked around with me like normal; he made no move to push me past what I was willing. It made me want to go further then I had said, but I kept that to myself. One step at a time.

That night I did indeed sneak into his room, which made it even funnier to us. I kept giggling and he kept shushing me to be quiet. Teasing that Millie would hear me and my cover as a scared little girl would be destroyed. We didn't do anything at all except laugh and go to bed. I hugged him and we fell asleep with my head on his shoulder.

It was about two weeks of sharing a room, when I decided I wanted to try and live with him as a wife should live with a husband. I was a little scared, but not how I used to be. I was just worried that it may hurt again or that I would not like it. I wanted to try though, and began planning how I would ask him or rather, how I would tell him.

We were already going to bed; he was in the washroom finishing up from the day. I left my housecoat over a chair and had taken off the bed slip so all I wore was my night gown. I took a breath and walked to the door.

He glanced up and stopped. He stood there half bent over, with water in his hands dripping through his fingers into the water basin. His face suddenly went very blank; I was not used to seeing the cautious look on him anymore. I wanted to get rid of it, but I didn't want to scare myself out of what I was going to do.

"Do you need this room, or." he paused and tried to keep his face calm. I could see thoughts behind his eyes, fears, worries, and hope. I smiled at that hope. "Did you want something else?" I knew his choice of words was deliberate.

"I was just wondering how much longer you were going to be. So I knew whether or not to stay awake or if I should fall asleep alone." I leaned my arms on the door frame and looked at my fingernails.

He knew by now that when I acted uninterested it was something that meant something to me and it was my way of hiding my thoughts. He dropped the water in his hands and started drying them on a hand towel.

"If my wife is tired, wants to go to bed, but not be alone. I can do nothing other than see her to bed so she is happy." He smiled at me. He walked towards me, as I stood with my attention on my nails.

He hugged me with one of his arms and stood back.

"Would you like an escort?" He asked as he held one arm out making me laugh.

"Why thank you soooo much kind sir. How would I have ever found my way?" I put my hand to my chest and laughed. He laughed and walked me to the bed. I saw him glimpse at the housecoat on the chair but he did not mention it.

After I was in bed he went to his side and got in, put his arm over for me to lie on. That was my Fredrick. Always willing to make me happy, never asking anything for him. I did not lie on his arm.

I turned towards him and propped myself up on my hands. My hair fell down my back, laid on the bed and his arm. I heard his breath catch before he looked at me. I smiled down at him and leaned in to kiss him. I kissed him deeply, he leaned up to kiss me back.

We said no words. I didn't need them and neither did he. He asked with his eyes and I answered with a smile. For the first time in almost seven months, we were truly man and wife.

Afterwards I started chuckling. He just looked at me and started laughing as well. He hugged me and I kissed his cheek. We fell asleep, and I had a nice long night without bad dreams.

We lived this way for another 3 or 4 months. My clothes were moved into his room. Millie began to tell me stories of her kids and asking me what I would do to my kids if they acted like hers. The house was finally a home for everyone. I was truly happy.

I stop writing once more. This time I debate pressing the delete button and erasing everything. These are my moments and I don't know if I want to share them with anyone.

I decide to leave them. If I died, I want Fredrick to live on. He was a wonderful person, I truly loved him, and I have loved few in my long years. Fredrick was the first, besides my parents, in my mortal lifetime. Also, seeing how much Fredrick and I loved each other, the life we had, that may just help whoever reads the story to see why He must be killed. It's not just a personal vendetta, Adam really is evil. My life is just a good example I realize, because I lived it.

Now it's time to write about Him. I never want to think of him, but I have to always. Until Adam is gone, my life will never be safe. I can never rest.

So I force myself to stop thinking about Fredrick and start remembering a part of my life I always try so hard not to. I have lived over one hundred years since Adam changed me. Through all that, the next part I have to write was the most heart wrenching memories for me. All the evil He exposed me to, all the suffering he made me cause. It all was somehow different than my next memories.

Chapter 7
A Fight

Fredrick and I lived together, as Husband and Wife with no problems. I could not believe how happy we were.

We had been talking about starting a family at the end of the year. Millie was even telling me I had better rest up if I was going to start working on a family. She couldn't wait to hear little feet in the house again. Life was finally working for us.

For a few days I had been feeling down. Nothing serious was bothering me. I could find no reason for my illness. I did not want to get up in the morning and I was anxious about everything. On the fourth day of this feeling, I went to bed early. I was feeling worse that night then the ones before it. I thought maybe I was just under rested and an extra long night may help me.

I lay down and fell into a troubled sleep. I had a foggy dream about flying, high bushes, trees. Things went by me that I had never seen, but I just flew by them. I felt like I was being chased and was also hiding. I was being hunted. I didn't know what was chasing me, but knew I did not want to get caught. I woke in the middle of the night with the dream fresh in my mind. It felt foggy, like a long lost memory that was fighting to be remembered. How could a dream of flying be a memory? Why did it feel real? What was wrong with me, to be feeling so unusual?

Fredrick was in a deep sleep beside me. I went to smooth back his hair and felt like I shouldn't. All of a sudden I was scared, I was feeling just like I had when we first got married. I took a deep breath.

'It's just the dream" I told myself. "You woke up from a bad dream and it lingers. You love Fredrick, why would touching his hair be bad?" I went to touch him again and found that I couldn't. My arm wouldn't move when I wanted it to. I could get no closer to Fredrick then I already was.

"Fredrick." I thought maybe talking to him would work. "Fredrick. Wake up please."

I went to move his shoulders but I could not make my arms move towards him. Each time they started to I would feel scared and pull away.

I got out of bed and went to the wash room. We had a small dressing area between the wash room and our bed chambers and I sat in the chair there.

"What is wrong with me?" I said aloud.

Nothing is wrong with you my dearest. Except that you got close to him

It took me a moment to remember the voice. I had heard it last just over two years ago. I couldn't remember why I knew it, but I knew that it had spoken in my head then as well.

"Who is there?" I would not speak in my head to a voice in my head. That was the stuff of craziness. If I was going crazy, I would not let myself go completely crazy before Fredrick and I could have our family.

Don't think of a family with him!

I tried not to think about the voice, but I suddenly remembered where I had heard the voice.

'My ball. I made you up so I wouldn't have to deal with the events of the evening. You are not real. So all I have to think about is what is bothering me now, that I would imagine you again.' I figured if I let the voice in my head that I knew it wasn't real, it would go away.

Oh no. I am real. You did not make me up.

I did not want to be going crazy. I tried to think of what could possibly be bothering me enough that I was hearing this voice again. What if it was the talk of a family? Was I really scared of a family? I thought it would have been wonderful to have a child.

Not with him

That one felt really close to me, like before the voice was down a hall way and now it was coming from the other side of a door. I could not think of what to do. I could not go near Fredrick to ask for help, but I was afraid of the voice more.

"I will help you my dear"

He spoke and when I looked up he was standing in the dressing room behind me, he put his hands on my shoulders like before. I tried hard not to react because to react to something that wasn't real was craziness, but I still felt like my skin was crawling.

"I come back to check on you, and I find you in bed with this man." I was shocked at how real his voice was. It was no longer a phantom voice. I had expected it to still be in my head even though I imagined him behind me. I looked at the opposite wall and tried not to react.

"I left to give you more time. To let you ripen into the woman that I remember. That I want. That I deserve after all these years dedicated to finding you again. I promised you on your wedding night that you would not be happy with this man. I had thought that if I had kept you apart long enough, that it would be safe for me to leave. I see now I was wrong. In my absence you have taken this human with you to bed." I felt the disgust in his voice and wondered why I would feel such disgust. For if I had imagined him then surely his feelings were my own. Were they not?

"I see now that I cannot leave you alone in this house, for you cannot be trusted. I promised you would not be happy with him. Yet you still tried to be. So I make a new promise to you. You dared to be happy with this Man." He leaned down and put his chin near my ear.

"I will not take you yet; I do not want your human to come looking for you. Instead, I will stay here. You want to be happy here?" he laughed lightly across my chin. "By the time I am done, all you would have brought to this house will be pain and tears."

With that he leaned further down and kissed my neck, again I felt a slight pain.

I dreamt of a small house. A feeling of emptiness inside me that was almost unbearable. I held a baby in my arms and smiled. I was so happy but felt so empty. I could not explain the feeling. It was like I had everything in the world, but nothing. I placed the baby in a small wooden cradle and turned around. I saw my husband. He smirked at me and walked over.

Something wasn't right, this wasn't Fredrick, but I could not remember who Fredrick was. There was only me, him, and our little girl. I closed my eyes to try and figure out what I was thinking.

I woke up the next morning in our bed. I remembered a dream of a house. The empty feeling in the dream had changed to a dread feeling in real life. I was just uneasy about everything. I didn't know what I was doing and was worried.

All day long I felt like I had when we first were married. Nothing felt right, I was not comfortable. Now, however I did not even find sanctuary with the help. Even with Millie, I was not comfortable spending time with or talking to. I stayed in the room all day and asked not to be disturbed because I was feeling down. I said my head was hurting and wanted to rest. I paced the room all day in fear of leaving it.

That night Fredrick came to the room, instead of going to the sitting room after dinner. He came to check on me and all I could do was sit in a chair and try not to shake.

"Tamson, I do not know what is over you today, but I want it to stop. You know that I ask little of you. However, this, this illness." He paused for the right words. "It seems to be nothing other than you avoiding the rest of the house and your duties as the woman of the house." At this I had to speak up, scared or not, I was actually offended for the first time since I had met Fredrick.

"My Duties! Avoiding? Since I have been here not once have I had to do anything, you never once told me to make sure something was completed? I have been sitting around just waiting for someone to pay me attention. I cannot believe that your mouth is uttering a word against me when I have done nothing but try to please you! Granted when we were first married I was withdrawn, but I worked on that my own. I came to you after I had worked it out. On my own. Since then I have done nothing but try to please you. So, I am sorry if, for once, I am not your perfect arm piece and had a problem I needed to be rid of by being alone for one day!"

Even as I yelled these words I was wondering what possessed me, that I would be so short with him. Just last night we had gone to bed early and fully enjoyed each other's company. We had been wrapped in each other's arms as we fell asleep thinking about the family we were trying to start, and today even his voice was vexing me.

I tried to apologize for being so rude, and to say maybe it was just my head ache. However, when I tried to speak my mouth only opened enough to sigh. I didn't know if it was me not wanting to apologize, or if it was simply lack of words, but he had words to say before I could figure it out.

"You speak of having to work though things on your own, but it was YOU who would not let me help. You speak of trying to keep me pleased and at that you have succeeded. I was pleased, but now I am not. I have never once done anything to make you feel like an arm piece. I took time to show you everything, and ask nothing. You have always been my priority. In doing so, I believe I have spoiled you. You are used to being the top of my list and are acting like a child now that things are not your way. I came up here to make sure you were well, before going out to check the lands. Seeing as you do not need nor want my help, I will leave you to fix yourself. While I check the grounds I have been neglecting, I want you to consider what you truly want from this marriage. If you even know, as you seem to change your mind often?" He started to turn and I called to him.

"Fredrick." I whispered as he reached for the door.

"What is it you wish for now Tamson? I, as you may or may not know, have duties to finish. Daily tasks that require attention. I will no longer neglect them because I love a woman who wants everything for herself."

His words stung. It was neither his mannerisms nor his normal voice. He was harsher, colder. It was as if the life had been taken from him and he was a hard shell that looked like my husband. I did not know why, but I could not stand the thought of him going out tonight.

"You do not need to go out tonight. Please do not. I do not feel well and ask this, for me, stay here." I whispered the words.

It felt like my voice was hiding from me, but I could not leave those words unsaid. I thought they would bring him back to me; instead they seemed to anger him more. My Fredrick was not an angry person. It scared and worried me to see him like this.

I was still overcome with dread at nearing him. Even though I could not go and hold him to me, nothing would stop me from trying to get him to stay inside tonight. Even if I did not know why I was scared, I had to try and keep him home.

"Tamson. Do you not see? It is all for you. Yet you still always ask 'for you'. I am going out to check the grounds and make sure all is well." He held up a hand as I started to protest again, "Tamson I have said my piece. You sit here with your choices. I love you, but I am not going to neglect my duties anymore. Not to try and keep you happy when you do not even know what it is you want. I just want you to know that everything I have done since I met you, was for you." With that he left.

I was scared and I did not know why. I knew that Fredrick had never spoken to me like that before. I wanted to go after him, but the sense of foreboding would not leave me.

I did not go to sleep. I paced the room. Worry sat inside me and would not leave. It was not the dread I had been feeling before, now it had turned into a feeling I had never known before. Like my life was over, I just had not found out yet.

My fingers stop racing over the keys and I feel a sigh escape. I swear it was a sigh, that wasn't one of those breathes you have when trying not to cry. I'm way too old to be crying over lost loves aren't I?

A thought enters my head about Derek and Mark earlier today. Had Derek's wife felt the dread I had that night? Did she worry about her husband when he was out late? Did some part of her love him so much she felt when he was in danger?

I feel tears well up again and shake my head. I will write this part down and have to stop stalling. I am writing to teach a lesson. I have to think of it as His story, not my memories.

I take a deep breath and start to type again.

Chapter 8
The Witch

Fredrick did not come home for a few hours. I was worried for him, I no longer felt uncomfortable, and I wanted to see him. Somewhere in me I felt a terrible premonition, though.

I called for Millie and had her send out a few men to search for him. It had gotten late and dark. The clouds overhead had turned dark and the wind had picked up. A few minutes after they left, the thunder started.

They returned to the house within the hour. His horse was found at the bottom of the ravine. They didn't want to tell me anything other than neither he nor his horse survived.

I cried out in anger.

I shook with sorrow.

I went insane with loss.

I screamed and cried out the pain I felt, until I felt empty inside. He never went out this late; he left because he couldn't stand me. I lay in my room just staring. Too spent to move, cry or even blink.

It was my fault my husband was dead.

I stayed up late that night. Staring into the fireplace, in the kitchen with a cup of tea that had gone cold hours before. I had told Millie that I could not sleep in our bedroom alone and that I would like my old room to be set up for tonight. Even though I stayed up all night, I did not see either bedroom. In the kitchen I sat, staring into nothing. I did not cry again after my initial screaming. The feeling of dread and discomfort was gone. I did not know if it was dulled from pain, or if I was just a bad wife.

Had I tricked even myself into being happy? Was I really not meant for Fredrick? I did not speak that night. I got up once to throw up cold tea in the servants wash room off the kitchen. After I sat back down, I stayed there until the servants woke and started the daily work that kept the house going. I did not want to see life go on, so I went up to my old room and slept the day away.

Fredrick's funeral was held two days later. I threw up my lunch when Millie tried to talk to me about the arrangements. The day of the funeral I threw up again when I was trying to get dressed. I held it throughout the service and then raced to the bathroom and everything came back up and I cried. The stress and emptiness was too much. I went up to my room after everyone left the house. I went to the chair by the window.

I remembered that it was not too long ago that I had sat in this chair and faked sickness to be away from my husband. Now I sat in this chair, looking out the same window, and would never be with my husband again. There was nothing left except cold loneliness and the knowledge that it was my fault. I looked at my reflection in the glass.

My hair was pulled back up on my head, but the back was left down. Millie had said that Fredrick had loved my hair down, and that I should not have it all up. My dress was all black, of course, nothing fancy, a few skirts and a blouse with long sleeves. A very small amount of lace at my wrists and collar. My mother had not made this dress; this dress was just one I had Millie go buy from a shop. I looked down in my lap at my fingers. I was too young to be a widow, but I thought I deserved it.

Fredrick did not though.

I had brought nothing but pain and false laughter to this house. I was the reason for everything bad that had happened. That was what I was thinking about as the sun disappeared.

As darkness rolled in slowly devouring the light, I felt no passage of time. Minutes felt like hours and hours flew by in seconds. I heard someone knock on the door, but I said nothing. I stared out the window into the dark. I was remembering the feelings I used to get at night.

When I was a child I had loved the night. I always felt at peace and more at home during the night. I could sit outside and everything felt peaceful. In my later teenage years I had felt the peace that should be there, but it felt out of reach. Like something was between me and the calmness of night.

Now, grown and widowed, I felt like the night was nothing. The night now held the same emptiness I had inside. I felt like everything out there was ominous and was watching me. Nothing was as it should have been.

I should have been with my husband, in our room. Happy.

I was just in a room. Nothing else to my future. Alone.

Not alone Little One. Never again

I closed my eyes and felt tears threaten. As soon as I heard that voice I remembered everything about it. It was at my debut. I heard it again on my wedding night. It came to me in dreams, even just a few nights ago.

My imagined man. Would I never be rid of him I thought to myself? Obviously he was here tonight because I could not cope with my husbands' death.

"What was wrong with me that I can not be in the real world? Why do I have to make up a person to deal with stress?" I wondered to myself. I would not acknowledge him this time. I knew he was not real. It was time for me to grow up and live my life. I was an adult, and a widow. I would have to become stronger then I was, and imagining things was not strength.

The voice came again after a little bit of silence from me. It was no longer in my head. At least, my mind made me think he was really in the room.

"You are mourning over nothing. You should never have been with him." His words stung. If I was making him up, then his thoughts were my thoughts. Why would I think, that I was not supposed to be with Fredrick? I had felt real love with him had I not?

"I told you that you would bring no joy to this house. You still tried to defy me. You let that Human touch you. Have you." The voice paused and when it spoke again, seemed closer to me in the room. I refused to turn around.

"I could not have that. I got rid of him so you would finally listen to me." I felt the first tear slide down my cheek. I did not hate when Fredrick was near me. I did not cringe when he would hold me. Why would my mind have this man say these things? What was wrong with me? Did all widows feel this way?

I felt the man's presence in the room now, no longer just a voice. I felt like there was a person behind me. I still refused to turn around; I would not give into madness. I wondered why he had visited this time.   Maybe if I followed the source of my worry, I could be rid of this phantom man. He moved closer to me and I still said nothing.

"You will no longer mourn him. I am here to be with you. To take you with me this time."

Was that it? Was my mind telling me I should leave. I was a bad wife. Surely I did not deserve to live in his house anymore.

Fredrick's Mother had not yet passed, she could take the house and I could leave. She spoke to me rarely and I hardly saw her anyway. She would not mind.

"Little one, I would have you look at me before I change you." I refused to look, I would figure this out and he would disappear. He said he was going to change me. How could he change me?

"If you will not look at me, or speak, then you shall feel the pain and feel all of the change. I will not soften it for you!" As he said this I realized that the 'change' he was talking about must be death.

My mind could not cope with this life, and brought my phantom man to bring death to me. I was actually, almost happy. If I could not be with my husband in life, then I would be with him in death.

"So be it!" He said and grabbed my arm, pulling me out of the chair where I had sat so calmly. It surprised me only slightly that I actually felt his hands on my arm, thoughts and imagination should not feel real.

I looked up at him calmly. I was ready to die. I would possibly go to Hell for the pain I caused Fredrick, but I was ready.

His eyes stared down at me and he leaned in. I thought he was going to break my neck or something but he bit me, hard. My knees buckled and I started to fall backwards to the ground, but he caught me. With a hand on my waist and one behind my neck he held me up as I let my fingers trail across the rug.

To this day I remember closing my eyes, awaiting death. Not being scared and thinking only of the way the rug felt against my fingertips and how I would follow Fredrick in death. I would finally be a good wife. I was not bothered at all.

"Do NOT think of him while I am touching you, think of me. I am your other half. You are mine, NOT his!" I did not know why he was mad, he wasn't even real. He was just my way of killing me without knowing it. He leaned in and bit again, harder, I flinched. I knew that this time I was really going to die. I closed my eyes.

I felt his lips leave my neck.

His hands felt lighter and he placed me back in the chair. He screamed in rage. I did not know what was wrong. Did I not know how to kill myself, was this some dream I could not wake from? Nothing made sense. I just sat and stared out the window again.

"Your blood tastes of him. You do not even know it. I got to take him before he even knew. I am glad of that at least, because he should never have touched you." He looked down at me in disgust, with something else floating in the backs of his eyes. A look that was fatherly, husband like, even kind and sad.

"I will not change you this night." At this I looked up in shock. I had wanted to die, why didn't he take me. I decided to speak, I was already crazy, and speaking it aloud would make no difference.

"You came here to kill me. Please, take me with you. I do not want this life."

He looked down at me. Something that almost looked like longing, love, and pain crossed his eyes.

"I remember how much you loved being a mother." he said which confused me, I was never a mother. However, some part of me thought it made sense, which confused me more.

"You may not want this life. However, I know how much you would love the life in your belly. I will give you the time to have the child. Even though he should never have touched you, I could never take away a child from you. I love you too much to do that. Know this, though, I give you this time, but you will know no other man. You will have the child, and I will change you then." With that he was gone.

I put my hand upon my belly.

"Life in my belly?" and I fainted.

The next morning Millie was waking me up, I had slept in the chair all night. She was worried that I might have died of a broken heart. I told her that I had thought I was going to.

"Millie, I had the most horrid dream and I thought I was dying. In the dream though, right before I felt death, I was." I paused; I did not want her to know I was crazy, but I had to explain my concerns. "It was almost like I was told by death, that I had life in my belly and I could not die until that life was started. Millie." I started to cry. "I think that maybe Fredrick and I have started a family, and he died before he was able to know!" I broke down and she held me, crying her own tears as well.

She told me that we could just wait and see, but that if I wanted to know right away, she knew someone I could go to.

"You must know Miss Tamson that not many people know of her, and those who do always feel fear in her presence. However, she knows much, and always helps. She can predict deaths, and lives, heal small sicknesses. Some say she can read minds and curse people. Some say she is a witch, but I have seen her. She frightens me, but I have never had trouble with her, and she helps. If I take you to see her, it must be after dark, for she is sickened by the sun.

You must also not speak of her to anyone, unless you feel she is the only one to help."

Millie was never this serious and in all our talks she had never mentioned seeing a witch. Nor had she seemed the kind who would have even gone to one.

I agreed and that night she took me to see this witch.

I stepped up to a door of a small house. It was hidden in the forest and had a large growth of plants hiding it from the eye. I could have walked by and not known it was there if Millie had not walked me straight to it. The place held such a sense of foreboding that I would have sped up my pace had I just been walking by. Millie had to tug on my arm slightly to get me moving towards it.

"I know what you're feeling, though I don't know why we feel it. She can help, I know that much."

For the sake of the lesson and time I have to write it down, I will cut this short. I feel Him nearing. This part of my life is not crucial to knowing Him. However, it is part of my mortal life that must be understood in order to see His wickedness.

The witch had Millie wait in the front room, and I followed the witch through a curtain. I was scared, but also felt at home. I told her of the dream I had, the man I had heard and seen. I was not scared of telling her. If she could read minds, then why hide anything.

She told me a few things, I will not write our conversations, but she did say this before she pulled Millie into the room.

"The visions you are having are truthful. You are with child. It is healthy, and I foresee you delivering and both of you surviving." She looked into a small box and sighed as she pulled out a small necklace with two small charms.

"However, I do see your death after the child is born. Do not tell anyone of your fate that I have spoken, or this fate may come before the child is born. I want you to take these." She handed me thin chain in my hand letting the charms touch first then dropping it completely. "Put this necklace on and never take it off while with child. When the child is born, put the necklace with the child and it will not be in danger. Later in life, it may be. This charm will help it find help." She called Millie into the room.

"She is with child, and it will be born healthy. However, if anything is to happen to Tamson after the child is born, it may be in trouble. I have given her a charm to wear while with child, the child will remember it. You take this second charm. If anything happens to Tamson, you come to me. Bring the child and the charm. I will help you protect it."

She closed her eyes. At the time I thought she was reading the future or something. I know now she was trying to find away to words things.

"Millie, if you do have to bring the child to me, you will have to change your life. It will be arranged and I will help you. However you must be willing to sacrifice your current life for this child, if need be. For it is important and must live on." Millie did not look scared and said she would do as asked.

"Tamson, after the child is born, there will come a time, when you have questions. You will not know where to turn. When that time comes, you will remember me then and only then, seek me out. I cannot help you, until you remember me on your own. After the child is born, you will not think of me until that time." She had me leave the room and spoke to Millie, who had been having back pain and wanted a tonic for it.

I sat in the front room with my hand on my belly staring at the necklace and charm. It was small and circular. Inside the outer circle was a shape similar to a cross, except the sides did not go straight out, they curved up and pointed. Almost touching the outer circle. The top of the cross stopped just above the middle, like it wasn't supposed to be there. Its edges also pointed up, just slightly.

I was healthy and happy the next eight and a half months. One night I awoke in agony. I felt like I had fallen asleep with a corset on and the boning was digging in. I realized that it had to be the baby and I called for Millie. By morning my daughter was born.

Evelynne Marie Godefrey was a perfect child. Millie helped in her birth and was the one who handed her to me. I cried as I held her and saw Fredrick's eyes staring up at me. I loved her with all my being. I did not want to die anymore. I finally had a part of Fredrick back, and his time I would love him properly.

I did not get the chance. He came back when Evelynne was only a month old. I had put her to bed. One of the maids in the house, Catherine, was also a mid-wife and was a perfect nurse. She was one of the first friends I had made here, after Millie. She was going to watch over Evelynne so I could rest that night.

I went to my room and was overwhelmed. It felt like the air itself was thick and heavy. I stumbled to the bed and sat down. My eyes were heavy and I squinted around the room. I thought I saw a shadow near the far wall before I fell on the pillow.

I pause for just a moment and close my eyes. I take deep breath to hold back tears, and start again.

Chapter 9
His House

I awoke in a new place. I looked around at my bleak surroundings. I was in an old stone room. It's ceiling higher than even a ballroom, so high that the only light was a torch on the wall with nothing upon the ceiling.

There was one window near the top of the wall that my bed was near. It was so high up that I could see nothing. I moved closer to the edge of the bed and could see stars out the top. It was positioned so that even on the other side of the room, I knew I would only be able to see the sky. A chair sat near a desk further down the wall my bed was on, and there was a door on the other end of the room.

I had no idea how I had gotten there, or where there was. I was feeling drunk and alert at the same time. I was overwhelmed by sounds and smells; I could see each crack in the walls, the threads in the bed linens. Seconds after I took in the room, I started to scream. If I did not know where I was, then were was Evelynne? Who had me, and who had her?

I heard footsteps outside the room and stopped screaming, I could hear it echo up the walls of the room. I huddled upon the bed scared and worried.

The door opened and in walked the man I had seen each time my life got to stressful. My first thought was that of course he would show up, what has ever been more stressful then this room? But then a thought crept into my mind as he stood there, how in the world can an imagined person open a door? He had always just appeared. Before I had time to think of anything else, he started to speak.

"My dearest. I am sorry to put you in these conditions. I am so happy to have you with me. Sadly, though, I am unsure as to your obedience, after the little incident of you being with another man. Being unfaithful to me, even after I had visited you, has given me due cause for concern. This room will ensure you learn to obey and trust me. You WILL stay on that bed during the day and sleep. If you do not, then you will be punished. You will learn to trust me as I will be the one bringing your food to you at night." He smirked at this.

I sat on the bed quietly, I had no idea what he wanted or if he had Evelynne or not. All I knew was that he was no longer a phantom. Either I had gone completely crazy, or he was real all along, because he was definitely real now.

"I would like to have you comfortable with me, but I must be convinced of you before I allow you certain freedoms. Good night." With that he smiled and closed the door.

I sat there all night. I would go through stages of crying and silence. I would pace the room or just sit on the bed staring at the window. It was dark out but I could see around the room. I wondered why he had said sleep during the day. Why would he bring me food at night? I was also wondering what punishment I would be given if I got off the bed during the day.

I found out that first morning. I was so scared, so anxious, that I was still awake when the sun came up. Vampires get lethargic, but can stay awake. Granted I did not know I was a vampire, I thought I was just tired from being up all night. So as the sunrise came nearer I thought nothing of it.

However, come sunrise, when it had risen just enough, I was shocked and scared. The sun came in that window, and I felt it. It was not touching the bed at all, I was in shadow. It did not matter. It felt like someone had lit a fire beside me, my skin was hot to the touch and my eyes stung. I had to close them and I hid under the blanket. I learned that if I moved off the bed after dawn, I would burn in the sun. The bed was put into the only place in that room that direct sunlight never touched.

It stung my eyes and skin so bad, from just seeing the light, that from then on I always was asleep before dawn. I made sure to be on the bed, and asleep so that I would not have to endure the pain. I soon realized that my body was healing each night before I woke. So anything burning that happened from the light, I would never know was there. As long as I slept the day away I didn't even know I was hurt.

I know now that the healing also used up some of my power, so it kept me weakened. From the first day he kept me weaker than him. He made sure he was always in control.

The second night I was there, he showed up soon after sunset. Smiling as he opened the door and saw me shying away from him. I was crying. I did not know where I was. I was missing my daughter. I was wondering if she was also here enduring any kind of weird torment, or was she safe at home. I was also scared because I did not know what was wrong with me, that I could not be in the sun. He had not brought me any food, he just came to check on me and he left.

He kept me in the room for days and nights without water or food of any kind. I couldn't even smell anything being cooked even though I could smell the sea and grass outside. I was hungry beyond anything I could ever remember. My insides felt on fire each night like I had never eaten in my life. On the fifth night I awoke hungry and worn. I felt as if I could barely move and prayed that he would not show and I could die. For surely even hell could not be this bad. That night however, he brought me something. He called it food.

I called it a child.

He had brought me a girl, not much younger then me. He said she was his own stock and I could feed freely.

I had no idea what he was talking about. He looked in my eyes and I faded into a dream. I was happy. We were all at a small river; my husband was trying to catch fish. I was watching a little boy splash around. Then suddenly in the dream I was eating. Just eating. The fish was the best I have ever tasted and I could not get enough. We were all laughing and I was just eating. When my fish was done I sat down on a tree stump and looked over at my husband. He glared at me with an evil smile. I blinked and we were not at a river. It was the barren rock room.

He was smiling at me, I shivered. I looked away and saw a girl lying on the floor. She had blood on her clothes but none dripped from her wounded neck. She had died. I looked down and saw blood all over my own clothes and his were spotless. He laughed and picked up the poor girl and left the room. As the door closed I heard Him say, "See, I told you she was hungry."

He kept me in the room, never leaving for just over a month. Then he slowly started letting me out of the room. Only with him beside me, and only for short distances. We would walk down seemingly endless corridors and end up back at my room.

He told me he did not have Evelynne. She was no longer my concern; she was with her human family. I was no longer human and so I could not see her. He told me many things and if I did not listen, I was punished. He would make me go longer between feedings, or bring me sick children. The one time I had cried and begged to see my baby, he had thrown me into my room and slammed the door.

The next night he brought me a pregnant woman to feed from. When I refused to feed from her, he snapped her neck in rage and left her there for two days on the floor. I wept so hard for her and her baby. I had heard its heart beat after she had died. It slowly stopped and I cried. He had made his point though, I never again asked about my old life.

He started telling me stories. Lessons he called them. Of my old life, of how I was his wife from the beginning of time. We were the original Vampires of the world. For the longest time we were the only ones. That after we had lived for millenniums, I had been killed.

When he had lost me, he could not stand being alone. The pain he felt on my death made him hate living. He found a way to lessen the pain, he made children. New vampires to remember me by. He made them to feel more complete but He was never happy he said. They learned our history, but were not me, and the pain was still there.

He told me of how he had searched for over a thousand years for a human to be born with my spirit and energy. A few lifetimes he had felt me enter and leave this world but had not been able to find me.

Now that he had me again, he would do all he could to protect and keep me. I learned little other then that I was supposed to be his wife. That I was his. He never told me what vampires really were, or how we were made. Never where I was, or what he wanted us to be. I knew that I was supposed to be his. Nothing else.

Soon after I stopped asking questions and began to just listen, he gave me more liberties. I was allowed to walk around, with him of course. But he allowed me to roam around away from my room and dark hallways. I discovered I was in a huge house. An older house made of stone, brick and in some places the walls were just carved rock. Like the house was built into the ground. I was not, however, allowed to leave the house.

I was never allowed to touch another man, he said. I fed from his poor victims, young girls. I learned that he kept some in rooms better than mine. They were allowed to see out their tiny windows. Not all of them were kidnapped but all of us were prisoner.

He had a few children that believed him to be their Father, but once they reached a certain age, they were food. Private stock he called these girls, when I asked.

"They taste better hand raised, the extra fear and confusion is delicious" He whispered as one girl skipped back to her room. I had learned not to cry in front of him, and bit my lip so I would not call out to her. I wept for all of them when I was in my room alone. I knew that one day I may see their faces when he had starved me and I had no control.

Some of the girls he brought me, and some that he fed from would survive. Either to be feed from them again, if it was his stock, or to let free with memories erased or altered. Those lucky few were also damned. They would always be scared of the dark but not know why.

He would bring them to us, read their minds to find their fears. He would have them live their fears in their minds as he fed from them. Claiming the fear made the blood flow stronger. He would cloud their memory just enough that would not recognize us or the place, but they would always have a fear they could not explain.

It was almost as if he didn't like killing them. He would leave them alive, afraid of him, even though they did not know it was him they feared. I saw that he was always for himself, and control. I hated him, but I could not resist eating when he starved me.

Sometimes he would not cloud their minds at all. He would let them see himself and I for what we were. Feed off them while they were awake and screaming, trying to pull away. He would bring me these meals after I hadn't fed for over a week. I would be starving and instinct would kick in, I would feed. As soon as I had their blood in me, my senses would return and I would be holding them. They were screaming in my face and he was smiling from across the room.

After I had been quiet and docile around him for awhile, He started to slowly let me have even more freedom. I was allowed into the gardens after awhile, and I mistakenly thought He was being nice.

After a few nights of visiting the gardens and allowed free roam, he asked me which my favorite spot was. I finally choose a place that I liked more than any other in the entire garden.

"Good, this is where we will rest." He told me. I was going to leave the room and no longer be burned by the sun each day. What should have felt like a blessing was a curse instead.

He found the one spot I enjoyed, and he took me down underneath it. He would never let me out at dusk. I remember thinking "He knows I would try to leave." I just couldn't remember anything about him, or us that would make him think that.

After that night, and my first day underground. He took me to a part of the house I had never seen before. It was a nicely built wing, but the decorations gave it a dreadful feel. I was taken to a huge bedroom. I turned around when I saw the bed. He smiled at me, the same smile he had when he made me feed.

"I told you, that you were mine. Now you will be, always." I tried to run.

I was already feeding off blood of humans. I was never allowed to see my daughter, he had told me she was alive, but how did I know. It could all be part of his sick game. He claimed to have killed Fredrick. This man ruined my life. I walked with him only because I had no idea how to survive without him, but I could no more endure the touch of him, then I could the glare of the sun.

He was faster than I could have imagined. I was thrown to the bed before I had time to scream. He was upon me with a hand over my mouth.

"Scream if you want, but you will be mine." He took me.

At first my body started to react to him. I felt a rush of heat shoot up my spine as he looked at me. At first, my body wanted him. However, my mind refused to give in, and my heart screamed in agony. Though my body seemed to hear his call, every other part of me rejected him. This was the man that was responsible for my husband's death, and mine. The man who had kept me away from my child with no knowledge of her life. The man that makes me kill girls and mothers.

As these thoughts ran through my head, my body stopped reacting; tears began to threaten my eyes. He started to touch me and my body found no pleasure in what he was doing. Memories and tears kept my body from finding any pleasure in what happened next. The less I reacted the worse he became. When I would cry out, he showed no mercy.

Even though I had been married and had given birth, it was worse than anything I could have imagined. He was without pity, and every time I would think it was over, he would start again. He would touch me in ways that were indecent, even if he had been my chosen husband.

I started to feel tears running down my face and he grabbed my hair, pulling my head back. He kissed and licked the tears from my face. I had a brief thought that maybe he would stop. I should have known he would never stop. As he finished licking a tear off my jaw, he pulled my head down and shoved himself inside my mouth. I couldn't scream or cry and it felt as if I couldn't breathe as my throat bruised under him. He did many things that night. Then just left me on the bed sobbing.

"You are mine." He said before he left the room. It was the first time he had left me alone, but I was too broken to do anything.

I was really broken. At one point, he had been hurting me more than I thought I could ever endure, I had tried pushing him off of me pleading him to stop. He broke my arms. Just pushed them both backwards until they snapped. I screamed out in agony as pain ripped through my body at both ends.

"They will heal." He said and kept going. I lay there bleeding and sobbing, and he finished.

He was ever watchful. He would take me to his room most nights, then back to our daily grave. Each day I would heal during our sleep. Sometimes he would starve me a few nights, then take me to the room and a girl would be naked and chained to the bed. After one of us killed her, he would take me. He would push me down upon her body, and I would cry onto her face while he took me.

I felt hollow inside. I began to just follow him around, knowing that my life was no longer mine, I was his. He enjoyed me and my body. He seemed to know I could not escape, so he stopped being so watchful.

As I started getting more freedom, my meals got worse. He would bring me young women my age, still virginal, and tell me if I did not learn to cloud their minds I would have to attack them to feed.

At first I could not do it, so he killed them in front of me, without even letting me feed. He would say they would leave with memories of us. Be a threat. I would starve until I could cloud the mind or attack without feeling. If I didn't learn to blur their memories, I would have to kill my food.

He sometimes took me to my old stone room and would leave me there with a sickened child. They would be too weak to fight me, or even kill me during the day. At night we would stare at each other. I knew he would not come back until they had died. I would try so hard to keep away from them.

One of them had made the mistake of thinking I was like them, and I awoke one night with her curled up beside me. I was so hungry and her blood teased my still drowsy nose. I awoke to her screaming and let go. She ran to the other side of the room and died crying. After that when he would take me to the room and leave me 'food' I would let them see what I was so they would not come close. A few died hiding under the desk, a few I was too hungry to resist. I learned how to cloud their minds slightly, but never told him.

He never actually helped me learn my abilities. He told me what they were and made me a situation where I'd have to try, but he never gave pointers. In fact, he kept me with him or locked in the stone room when he went out; to make sure I stayed as human as possible even with my powers.

The times I was allowed to be alone, there was no one to use and nowhere to practice. I had noticed that he could do much more than me. While he pretended to 'teach' me things, he seemed happier when I could not do them. I began practicing to do things I had seen him do. Since he thought I was broken in, he would leave me alone some nights. I would work then.

I had slowly been regaining my memories of my former lives. Though I did not know what they were at the time. Sometimes I did not know the specific place, but I would remember bits and pieces. Sometimes I would get De-ja-vu when he would say something.

Each time I learned a new power or skill, I would remember an instance of using it before. Maybe not what I was using it for, but I would remember the feelings and would not have to practice it to perfect it. Things just came back to me. It was like once I learned the basics, the full power was learned. I kept them hidden though. I would show him a few things I learned but stumble through them so he felt I was less then I was.

The first skill I remembered this way happened one night when he left me alone and I felt him leave the house. I was alone in the stone room. I spent all night trying to jump more than a human could. When I finally succeeded, I reached the window in one bound. I had remembered running from someone, and jumping up to the top of a building. I ran afterwards, not looking back. I remembered feeling the wind in my face and hair.

I let go of the window and fell to the bed. I didn't know how to slow myself down and landed hard. It didn't hurt, but it was disappointing after such an achievement. I lay in the bed remembering the wind in my hair, not the jump, and wished I had space to learn to run like that.

I was with him a full year, with increasingly more evil things done to me. Saw so many deaths, hurt so many people. I will skip the other horrors I had to endure, and write down the events of the last night I was with him.

Chapter 10
A Play

I was remembering more and more of myself and of him. I knew that we really were together in a past life, and that he was not this bad before. I never let on that I was remembering though. In my last life, I had been planning to leave him, He just never knew. In this life I was waiting for my chance to complete those plans.

He had finally decided to take me out. However, he had a way of perverting such a delight like always. I was to go with him to a play. His idea was to make me choose one of the actresses on stage. She would be my dinner. I would make this play her last. I was already appalled and didn't want to go, but I was afraid of what he would do to the actors if I didn't cooperate. So I had gone along.

We went to the last showing of the night, it started an hour after dusk and would be over right before midnight. He sat me almost to the front so I could see them in detail. I was partially grateful because the theatre was so full of lust and hormones it was hard to breathe. The front near the stage was full of excitement and confidence. The actors loved their jobs, playing risqué parts was a challenge for them. It didn't matter to them that their show was a meeting ground for illicit affairs.

Now that I look back on it, he was making me select from them as humans would later choose lobsters from a tank. He would not let me just point and leave though, I was to sit and watch the play so I could appreciate my prey.

If he had let me leave, then maybe my life would be different. If we had just chosen and left, maybe I would still be with him, maybe the world would be safer. Then again, it may have been more dangerous. I don't know. I do know, however, that staying caused me to leave him sooner than I would have been able to, had I left without watching the play.

We sat down and some soft music started up, it was a small play. One I'd never heard of. The curtain opened to a small garden like setting. The actor and actress were dressed in cloth so closely colored to their skin it almost looked as if they were nude. I heard a few small gasps in the audience; apparently to human eyes they did look nude.

They started speaking, the voices carried to the back of the audience, but you could tell that they were speaking in whispers. I was so caught up in the fact that the whispers could carry that I wasn't listening. The actor was looking around and she was holding something in her hand. He nudged me and asked if I liked her. I stared at him and realized I had forgotten why I was here. I tried not to get attached in any way to prey, but I had with these two.

"No I don't think I do." I replied, "She does not appeal to me."

"Then just enjoy the show until the next possibility arises. I hear this is a very controversial play. It's supposed to be about the worst sins of man. It sounded amusing."

I started to pay attention to the words then, I had been taught about sins from my mortal parents, and seen more sin in the past year then I wanted. Sin on stage however, I could not imagine what they would do. The actress was chewing on something and had handed the object to the man. I realized they were playing out the first sin of man, Adam and Eve, eating the apple in the garden.

As I watched I saw shame float onto the face of the actress as she saw her husband's flesh. I marveled at the actress's face control but something began to nag at me.

"This isn't right." I whispered knowing only he would hear me, "Something about this doesn't feel right." I kept watching. He asked me what felt wrong. He was worried. I did not notice then, at the playhouse, but afterwards. He was wondering if I was remembering my past.

"I don't know, just something feels wrong. It is how I was taught, but it seems wrong somehow." Before he could utter a word I had a flashback, it was only a second of time. I did not have the long flashbacks of today's movies, but a single instant where my mind remembered everything.

I remembered the beginning of my first life, my mother, my first home. I remembered that the man beside me was my husband. I also remembered when I had loved him.

I remembered our sin.

Our children

Then I remembered our death, the cursed life that followed. I remembered my skills, my strength, and my determination. I even remembered life without corsets and rules. I knew I could break free of him. I had also remembered the control to hide all this from him.

"Never mind." I said before he could ask anything else. "I think it's just the way they're speaking. It's not the way I was read the story." I went back to watching the show, and so did he. It was no longer important.

It wasn't real anyway. It had triggered a memory in me, of the real original sin, and all that followed. I replayed it in my head over and over. He watched the play, and I remembered our lives.

Before I tell you anything else, or can even explain our life, I should go back a bit more then I can remember to explain our beginnings. You see, it's not that I never remembered this; it's just events that happened before I was born at all. I was taught of the beginning. All of our beginnings, the beginning of all things.

There was only One. A life force of ultimate power. After existing for so long this One became lonely. Separating some of its own power, the One, the Creator, sent out three bundles of energy to mature in stars. The star closest returned with the ability of divination, and spoke to the Creator about a problem. Something was wrong with the second bundle, but it was not yet known what that was.

When it returned to the Mother, they were shocked. The being was slightly different; they had to come up with a name for the difference. The One decreed that they were of her; she was their Creator, and therefore the Goddess Mother. They in turn were Goddess Foresight and the God Ahman.   Thus   the difference between female and male was started. He seemed to have all the powers they had. Nothing was wrong except he looked different. So it was not thought upon anymore. The third bundle came back as a young goddess, who controlled the unknown and the more chaotic feelings of the Mother.

The Creator looked upon Foresight, Ahman, and Chaos and smiled. Foresight was to be the Sun and Chaos was the Moon. Ahman was to be the Physical while the Mother would be all around. She would no longer be lonely for she always had family now.

Foresight came to the Mother and told her of danger. She had seen betrayal, pain, and death. Foresight spoke of a darkness that would cover herself, and then work through Chaos to get to the Mother.

Soon, or rather soon in the life of a Goddess, darkness did spread. Ahman had formulated a plan to take Foresights power, overtake the Mother, and take Chaos as his own. He asked Chaos to speak with Mother.   While they were talking, he over took Foresight and devoured her energy. He had an instant vision from Foresights power, darkness covering the Mother. Ahman believed he would drown out her light. Unfortunately for him, he read the vision wrong. The darkness he had seen was Mothers own anger. Chaos told Mother that he had asked her to come to her. The Mother remembered the prophecy and knew that Foresight was already part of him.

She protected Chaos from his eyes and set her own trap for the Ahman. When he came to hopefully take over Mother, he was caught. She could not forgive him for destroying Foresight, but could not bring herself to destroy him. She created two forms on the physical planet that had been his realm.

They resembled the God and Goddess's of the Heavens, and she separated his powers between herself and them. She took Foresights power from his and split it between herself and Chaos. Visions were never solid and therefore not needed. She took his energy and put it into the two forms, and breathed life into them.

They were the first.

We were the first.

We were Vampyr.

She had created 'Adam' and 'Eve', from the essence of a disturbed God. Adamah and Sa'ara.

The man sitting next to me and myself.

The Adam and Eve I was watching on stage, they were how Humans had tried to remember us. No wonder he found this funny to watch. I knew why it felt wrong.

They blamed me.

Chapter 11
Birth of Vampires

Our original sin had been worse, I think. Our punishment was worse than humans could imagine.

We lived with no worries in the beginning. We were not gods, but we did have some powers. We were fast, had excellent vision during day and night. I guess we were similar to the super heroes I hear kids talk about. Everything was easy, because we could do things easily.

Although, we always had to work for our food. Humans like to believe that, until the first sin, everything was handed to them.

No, we had to till the ground and hunt our food from the beginning. It wasn't a punishment; it was just to make sure we appreciated everything. We had powers over the earth and animals to make it easier, but having to do some work was never a bad thing.

The only thing Mother asked was that we drain the blood from any animal we killed. Since blood was the life force, and she created life, we had to offer it up to her as thanks. It was not hard and it was easy to understand. We gave her back the life that we had taken. She gave the animal life, we took the life so we could live, and we give her back that life in thanks. Simple. Little did I know that my husband did not find it so simple.

One day he came to me and spoke close to my ear, "Why do you think we have to offer the blood to Mother?"

I looked at him in shock, I thought he was kidding and teasing me. The look on his face was one I had never seen, and I realized he was serious.

"We thank her for our life, by giving her the life we took, back to her. Why would you even ask?" I replied. It was the first time I had to question my husband, and I felt confused and worried.

"I think that is just a story, an excuse. I think that she knows that is the best part of the animal, and she tells us it is 'thanks' so she doesn't have to share. If she is taking this blood, and she is even more powerful than us, then the blood must have some power giving ability." He must have seen something on my face because he stopped and looked down, "It is just something I was thinking about. I wanted to talk about it, is all. Do not worry" With that he turned and walked away. I thought about calling to Mother and telling her, but was afraid she would think I was questioning her, so I didn't. All was fine until a few months later.

We were putting out the blood for thanks. It had just been a small animal, similar to a deer today, but smaller. There was no real ritual, we just drained the blood, then stuck it in a cup or bowl for her to take with her after she visited. This day, however, he turned to me before we walked away. He had a similar look in his eyes as when he questioned me. It was almost as if thoughts that weren't his, were behind his eyes.

"I want to taste it." He whispered to me. "I just want to know if it does give her the power or not. How do we know that she doesn't make us give it to her, because it gives her power over us? If we taste it and nothing happens then we will know, but what if we drink and we gain power. I don't want to be her lesser if she's forcing us to be."

"You cannot drink the blood we give her. She gave us life; it would be horrible to do this behind her back. Why don't we just ask her about it?"

"Do you think she would really tell us? If drinking the blood would make us as powerful as her, she would keep it secret. She likes to have someone look up to her and never question her. If nothing happens then I know she is truthful and I will be happy. If something does happen though, then we can decide what we want to do, be whatever we want. No. I will not ask because I cannot trust without proof. We will just sip very quickly. If nothing happens we will go back to life. However, if we do grow more in power, imagine the possibilities."

We argued back and forth in hushed voices. As the sun reached its highest point in the sky, I told him he could taste but I did not want to. We walked back to the cup. He picked it up and put it to his lips. I saw him swallow and went to leave, but he grabbed my arm.

"Please, for me, just one drink. That way we can live together still and I will always have you. I do not want to gain power without you by my side."

I just looked at him and gave in, I knew he would not drop it, and I was wondering if he really was changing. Doubt is a powerful persuader.

I turned and he held the cup for me. I tasted just a little bit, almost less than a sip. It was a little sweet but tasted odd to me. I didn't feel any more powerful but I did feel a little sick. I looked away and he let me leave. He cleaned off the top of the cup and we left.

That night when we were eating, Mother came to see us. She did not always visit; one day is mere moments to the heavens. I felt it a bad sign and sat quietly.

She asked us if we were doing well, and was pleasant. She stayed with us for some time, and all seemed to be fine. Then she turned to him and asked.

"My son, did anything different happen today?" She showed no sign of knowing, but I could feel that she did. I hung my head and waited for his reply.

"Nothing Mother. We spent the day together. A nice day. Thank you for the clear skies and good harvest." I didn't feel any more powerful so I knew the blood we had drunk had done nothing to us. I couldn't believe he lied to her. Maybe things would have been better if he told the truth, but he didn't. All at once you could feel the absolute power that she wielded. She held herself and just let her power spill out to us.

"My children. My own body and my own power." I didn't look up but I felt her look at me as she spoke again, "Are you sure nothing happened today that I should know about my Son?" I kept my head down. I could not bear to see her eyes when he told her.

"Mother, I would not keep secrets from you. Nothing today seems noteworthy, or important enough to repeat really." At once her power disappeared, she diminished somehow. I could not believe he lied to her still. Did he think since nothing happened, it didn't happen? Did he grow in power and I was the only one unaffected? What would make him believe she did not know?

"Look at me both of you." We both looked up at her. I could already feel tears in my eyes. He stood as if nothing could harm him. I wondered if the blood had worked on him and not me. She spoke slowly and thoughtfully.

"Please do not speak. I must say this and be done. You must know, that I know, that today you drank of the blood you are supposed to give me as thanks. Even if I had not seen you, I can sense it still in your bodies. I had hoped that you would not be like him, but you still thought to maybe challenge me, or at most, gain more power. Just as my first son had. I can see that this may all have been a mistake, I should have destroyed Ahman. However, I have grown to love you two as I love my own. I will not destroy you, for to do so would destroy part of my heart. Instead, you shall always pay for this, this sin against me. You were not happy with your lives, you sought against me." She sighed, and I knew she was saddened.

"You shall have twenty years. These years are to have children. These children will look like you, but be different, they shall be Human. They will have no power but that of life and the ability to grow. I will not bless them as I have you, they will not see me nor talk to me. They will feel me when I am near, but will not know me.

"Your punishment is not over there. During the twenty years you will not age, but you will lose all your powers. This is so, as your children grow, they know nothing about you. If you speak to them about me or how you were made, they will die.

"At the end of these twenty years, you will fall asleep at night, and die yourselves. However, in the middle of the night, you shall arise again. Neither as a simple Human nor blessed Vampyr. You will be Vampire. You will still be immortal, you will have your abilities back, but you will be changed.

"Since you drank blood to challenge me, you shall survive only on blood. Human blood, the blood of your children, will be the only blood that sustains you properly.

"You drank blood when the sun was at its peak, so you will only walk in the night. The sun will now burn your skin and sting your eyes.

"Your punishment for distrusting me, for going against me, will be to lose me. You will no longer feel my presence, even though humans can.

"You will not know if I am near or not, you will not see nor hear me. I could be in front of you and you would walk through me and not know.

"Because your children can feel me, and I am gone from you, they will be afraid of you as Vampires. They will feel you are different because they will feel my absence inside you on a basic level they do not understand.

"I cannot bear to lose you, cannot destroy you, but can see that the freedom I wish to give my children is not good for them. When free, you seek to become more. Your children will be free but will not have the means to be more. Your children are my children so I will look over them.

"You however, you will be returned to your powers, but cursed. As Vampyr, you are powerful, you know me, and you live forever. As Vampires you will be cursed, limited to only blood and darkness. You will be powerful, but with only each other.

"Humans will fear you. Though you will be immortal again it will be an eternity without me. I am sorry it came to this, but I cannot allow anything more to happen. I loved you and Love you, but this is my decision. I am sorry." She sighed and looked at me, "Goodbye."

And with that she was gone. Gone from our house, and gone from our bodies. I felt like a hole was ripped in my chest. I fell to the floor and gasped once before a horrible sadness came over me. When I finally looked up he was still standing there as if he was not harmed.

Had the blood really changed him? Was I the only one without power and therefore the only one cursed? What was happening?

"She seeks to scare us. We still have our powers, she has just dulled them, so we will obey. I see the blood does not give power, you were right in that. I am sorry she is doing this, but it will be over soon." I think he really believed that. That we were cut off from our powers, for only a short time not forever.

It was exactly one month later that it happened. We woke and I was covered in blood. Not from any wound we could find. He blamed her, said it was a cruel joke to remind us that she had power when we didn't. I went to the river to clean off I walked back home and he looked up and asked why I hadn't cleaned off properly. I looked down and saw blood all along my legs I thought she had changed her mind.

"She said I would live twenty years! She can't change it, I don't want to die." I don't remember anything else; I just woke up lying in our bed.

"You fell down like you were asleep. I don't know what is happening but the blood has not stopped. I can find no blood from me. I can only hope that she takes us both for I cannot be without you." He held me close and we fell asleep together. After a few days the blood finally stopped, we had no idea what was happening.

He did start working harder thought. Without powers the cold night air stung and the sun burned out skin so we started making bigger animal skin covers. Our small house had many drafts I had never noticed before, so we started making the walls thicker and more solid. Before we had to work, but not his hard, and we never tired this fast. Now we had to do more, and I knew our powers were not returning.

In the next months neither of us found blood on us anywhere. He stopped draining the blood from the animals he now had to chase down for food. He said if she wanted to play silly games and take our powers and torment me, then he didn't want to thank her till she returned our powers. I still felt that if he hadn't lied that she might not have done it, so I always said a quick thank you to her before I ate.

Which was a lot.

I began finding all kinds of food, I would walk under a tree and smell the fruit and have to have it. He began finding different seeds that planted right would grow and we could eat. I thought maybe I was eating too much because my middle was growing. I was having trouble sleeping, and then some nights I would sleep too long. He became mad at me and I would cry for hours. I thought she was punishing me even more for something, I just did not know what.

One night after a few more months of my middle growing, I woke in pain. I felt wet and cold all over and thought I was covered in blood again, but it was sticky water. I looked around but when I went to stand pain shot through me. I grabbed him and told him she was taking me. He sat by me and cried while pain grew inside me. He kept saying it wasn't fair to take me from him, that we should both go or both stay. At day break I was still there, still in pain, but it had moved.

"It feel like I must empty myself, but the pain won't let me move. I cannot get away from here. Please go get the bowl we used for blood so I can empty. I cannot take the pain and this." He went to get the bowl and I felt like I would explode. As he came back in, he dropped the bowl. I asked what was wrong.

"No. I mean, I do not know. I do not know what this is. Something is inside you." He paled in skin and came over to hold my hand.

"There is something coming out of you, in the spot I do not have." I cried again and tried to push it out. If there was something in me I wanted it out. I would not die as deformed as I was, and have something inside me.

As I pushed the pain grew but also faded. I felt something and asked him if it was out. He went down to look and his eyes went big.

"Try again. It is still in but I cannot explain what is out. Just push it out. Hold on for me, and help me get this out of you." I threw my head back and cried. I pushed thinking that my silence must have been worse than his lie because everything was happening to me.

Finally I felt like it came all the way out. He dropped down and caught it and slowly stood up, holding a huge bloody animal. A cord was hanging down. He put the animal on my stomach and asked me to push again. I felt something else come out and the pain disappeared. I looked down and saw my middle was back to normal, though very soft. The animal that had been inside me was not moving. I went to touch it and it rolled and I saw its face.

It looked like us, not like any animal I had ever seen. A small rounder version of us. I knew we didn't have a cord, so I told him to take it off. He grabbed his skinning knife and cut the cording connecting it to the bag of blood that had come out after it. It started to drip blood so we tied it in a knot. I began to explore the face and noticed it wasn't breathing like us.

I looked up scared and he picked it up, he smacked its back and cleaned out its mouth and it made a horrid noise. Once we had missed a bird and just hurt it, while we had hunted for food. It had screamed in pain and this was similar. He put it down and backed away; I just started at it and understood.

"These twenty years are to have children. We are her children; she made us of her power. But our children, we have to make, and we have no power." I looked up at him, "We have to make them with our bodies. Since I'm made after her, I have to create the Humans. She is not teasing us. We really are being punished. This is the first Human, our first child."

I looked back down as he walked towards our child. He picked it up and it quieted. He came over to me and I reached out. My child lay in my arms and was silent. I looked down and she looked up and I smiled. My daughter, our daughter.

"I made her." I looked up at him and we kissed but I felt pain again. This time in my chest. I looked down and she had me inside her mouth. Her hand was on the opposite side like she was holding me. The touch gave me a tingle and something fell out of that side. He reached down and picked up the drop on his fingertip. He put it to his lips and tasted it.

"I do not know what it is but it doesn't taste bad. It must be what she needs to eat." We looked down at our daughter and felt the first happiness we had been allowed since the Mother had left us. I was still empty inside, but happy as well.

My mind was brought back to the play when he tapped my shoulder and asked if I liked the new actress. I felt a tear move down my cheek. It was from the sadness of the memory, the remembered life, and the knowledge that none of my children from those twenty years was alive. I had one child left, and he had made me leave her behind. He saw the tear and took that as my choice.

"Yes, I know you do not like to pick your food, but look at her, a fine delicacy. Not too big, with meat on the bones. She will be a fine meal. Now you can watch the show and enjoy it, we will eat when it's done." He went back to ignoring me and laughing at the ignorance of humans.

I had remembered everything. Everything. I decided right then that I would call him Adam. I knew his real name, and knew I was the only one alive who knew it. At least when I had died the first time, no one knew it other than me. I would never speak his name aloud again. I would call him Adam, the name our human children had given him.

While Adam watched the play, I began plotting my escape. The entire time I had been with him, he had told me that he had learned his powers and would teach me when I was ready.

Now that I had remembered, I knew it was a lie. We had learned how to control our powers together. Some I had even helped him to learn, or perfect. We had learned them together, and I still knew them.

He taunted me throughout the rest of the show, waiting till the end when, he believed, we would be taking a life. Every time the actress was on stage he got anxious, asking me sick questions, debating what part of her to feed from. He would ask me how I enjoyed her final performance. Little did he know that she would be the first I saved from him, and tonight would be his final night with me.

After the show was over and the audience began to leave, we went out to the entertainers entrance/exit. He spoke to mellow, to stay back and he would bring her to me, that way I would not mess up and let someone see us. So I stayed back, far enough away that I had room.

When they came out he blurred the minds of the other actors, with thoughts of her walking off down the alley. He grabbed her and started toward me. As Adam turned to bring her to me, I braced my feet. He would feel a power attack, but I had also remembered the martial arts I had learned ages ago.

He released the actress' mind, so she would know what was happening. Before he had found my mortal body, he had grown to like anguish. I remembered that before I died he was growing more and more mean, but he had never been this bad.

Since my death he had grown to like knowing that he scared his prey. He almost fed off their fear as well as their blood. I claimed her mind so she wouldn't remember this night, as I jumped up and kicked at his head.

He realized a moment before I would have struck him and he dodged but I still landed a good hit on his left cheek. He reeled around to face me as I struck out and landed a punch on his right shoulder. I struck out with power as well and pushed my fist through till I heard bone crack. He leaned to the right. He was prepared for feeding and scaring, not fighting.

As he went to stand back up I swept right to left and took his feet out from under him and with power pushed down on his now hurt shoulder. He started to drop but twisted and caught himself with his left arm and looked up with red in his eyes.

"Why are you doing this to me?" He asked, "Why are you hurting me when I saved you from a mortal life and brought you back to yourself?" While he spoke he was pushing with his power, thinking I was still weak with inexperience.

"Because this is all your fault." I said striking out again, feeling tears in my eyes.

"You lied in the beginning." I pushed my power around him on all sides. "And you've been lying to me." As I said this, I worked up all the anger and hurt I felt.

"I could have been happy as a human!" I remembered loving him at one point, and remembered the moment I stopped loving who he was. I sent that moment of memory into him. As he realized I was no longer his,

"And I'm leaving." I said as I pushed all my power into him along with a knife shaped hand down on his neck. He fell down and was out, but I knew from that he would soon be up. He had not eaten yet tonight, but he was still powerful.

With the last of my power I took the girls memory away and replaced it with one of walking down here and leaving safely. She would recall this night as the other actors would, but in the morning she would want to leave this city and find a new job. I didn't want him to hunt her down in revenge.

I jumped up to the building top and looked down at him. The man I had once loved, had lost, had hated. This man was all that was wrong in my life, and I was leaving.

I could already feel him working his way back to consciousness. I didn't have it in me to kill him, but if I was near when he woke he would do so much worse to me.

I turned and ran over the roof tops. It had been ages since I had the power and freedom to do anything. The human I was raised as was afraid of the heights. I had been told me that humans would die from a fall this high.

But I wasn't human, I never really was.

I was a vampire.

Originally a Vampyr.

I was the mother of every human on this world. That did not matter anymore though. All that mattered was hiding me from him until I could figure out what I was going to do.

Chapter 12
Failure

After that night I traveled the world, visited every town I had ever heard of or read about. I revisited places I had been to with him. After I had remembered our life together, I knew how to save my assets. I was able to blend in well each time I stopped moving.

I traveled to the Far East, and to the new worlds. Each place I went I assumed a new name, a new role, and a new life. After I had been there for awhile I would sense his energy getting closer, so I would move around for awhile. I knew he was hunting me down. I knew I was not safe from him, but it still took almost a year for me to figure out what to do.

I would train. When we had lived together as vampires, we had learned a few human skills. Mostly out of boredom, and my curiosity. He didn't like them though; he relied on his powers more. If I spent my time focusing on perfecting my powers, and training my mind and body, maybe I could defeat him. If I was able to kill him, and rid the world of his touch, maybe I could finally find peace.

What I did not know, was how to start training. Who could I go to? As soon as that thought entered my mind, I knew who to go to. I traveled back to my mortal hometown. I realized that I should have come here first and tried to find out about my daughter, but I was so intent on getting away from him I had just ran. I also think part of me had forgotten her in defense. I was a little ashamed of myself for not breaking free of his mental chains as well as his physical ones.

I went back to my old house, I wondered slightly if anything was still in my name. How they had explained my absence. Were they even alive? Had he killed them all? It was less than two years ago that I died. It was possible that everyone was still alive and still in the house, but I kept walking.

I retraced the steps Millie had taken me on and went to see the Witch. She had said to seek her out when I had questions, and I had questions.

I found her still there. She smiled sadly when she saw me. We talked until it was almost light and she took me down stairs where she had sun free rooms set up. She was not a witch. She was a vampire as well. I fell asleep that day with a mission in my mind.

I stayed with the Witch for a month. The first night I found out much. She told me how she had been made by a vampire, not Adam though. He was one of Adam's 'children'. He had made her to be his female consort. He was exactly like his vampire father. Evil and malevolent. He thrived on the pain of others and forced her to participate when he would 'play' with his meals.

She had escaped and vowed to help humans as much as she could. She used her senses and powers to figure out what was wrong with humans and help them fix it.

I found out that Adam had changed and taken me in one night. Millie found that I was missing and came to the Witch that night. Together they concocted a story that I had just left. A rumor was spread that I missed Fredrick so much and the birth of our daughter helped my depression take hold.

I left because the memories were too much. Evelynne was made the ward of Fredrick's Mother, but she had fallen ill three months after my disappearance. She had made Millie the guardian of Evelynne and the entire estate would be hers when she was old enough, or married.

The Witch had told Millie that I was not just missing, but I had been taken away. That I may return, but those who took me would always be near. If Millie tried to find me she and Evelynne may be in danger. As long as the necklace was near Evelynne and Millie kept the charm on her, they would be left alone. However, if I sought them out, I could cover my tracks so they would not be put in danger. The charm I had been given by the 'witch' was made to protect from the eyes of evil. So the man, who chased me, would not come for them.

After two nights, I decided to visit the house. Millie was up late in the kitchen. I saw her through the window and she looked much older than when I left. I knocked lightly on the servant's door. She came to it and paled when she saw me. Without fear she reached out and pulled me into a hug.

"Miss Tamson I knew you would return. Oh, much has happened since you were taken." She started to pull me into the house, but I stopped her.

"Millie, I want you to know something before I enter." I paused, afraid of her reaction, and debating how to say it.

"The man, who took me, has made it to where I cannot visit again for a long time. I have been changed, I am now like the Witch, and I am hunted." I started to explain more but she held up a hand.

"Tamson, I know more things than most, but I know there are things I will never understand. I feel the fear I feel around the Witch, but I know neither of you would hurt me." She smiled at me, "Whatever has happened to you, and her, I know it is evil. But I also know that both of you are good, and will fight it. Now come. Evelynne is sleeping and will not be able to feel the fear. You must see her!" Millie pulled me upstairs to Evelynne's nursery.

My daughter was lying in her crib. Red hair splayed out beneath her head. She stirred as we walked in and I almost left thinking she feared me. But she smiled softly and I fell down to my knees beside her. I felt a tear slide down my cheek.

I decided right then, I would not kill him for my peace of mind. I would kill him for her. For Fredrick. For the Witch. For all the lives that were ruined because of his evil.

That night I stayed in the house and walked through all the rooms people were not sleeping in. I wrote Evelynne a letter and gave it to Millie to give to Evelynne when she was older. I went back to the Witch's house before dawn. I stayed a few more weeks, planning my course of action.

She told me a few places I could go to train my mind and body. I told her that I would travel east first, and go to the mountains where I could be away from big cities and learn to calm myself. I did not want fear setting in when I had to fight him. We agreed I should not go back until I had defeated him. Evelynne was in capable hands and I could do nothing else for my mortal family. If I came back here, if my path led him here more than once, he would know. The charms could not protect them if evil is purposely looking for them.

Then I left to start my journey. I left to start training. I left to kill Adam.

I traveled long and fast. I made my first stop in Tibet. I met with monks and the Dalai Lama. I learned how to calm the body, and train the mind and soul. I had to leave before I wanted. I had not fully finished my training, but was forced out because the British were trying to take over. I could not be near all the bloodshed, because I wanted to help, but could not risk being found out.

I then traveled to Japan and learned the sword and Ninjitsu. I stayed as long as I could as I studied different forms and styles. In the early 1900's I traveled to the United States. I found that I could travel to different parts of the States and hide well. There I learned to fight, boxing style. I disliked it, but thought that maybe it would be a style he would not know. I left for South America when a world war broke out. I did not want to be anywhere that was high profile, as I was sure he was behind this somehow.

I was learning more and more about defense. I kept traveling, and even took a few trips to places for fun. I went to see Paris, which

I had wanted to visit since I was mortal. There I learned about fencing so I did not feel like I was wasting time.

Near the end of the 1970's I headed back to the Americas. I stayed in South America for a few years, just moving from place to place, because I felt him getting closer. It was then that I realized he was closing in on me, and I would not have time to train anymore, just to plan.

I moved up to the United States in 1985. The cities were getting higher in violence. I knew I would be able to eat well, and hopefully hide better then in forest regions. I studied a few gang fights. Seeing if there was anything in the fights that I could use. I started practicing my styles in apartments. I could not risk being seen outside fighting, in case he was masking his presence.

I melded different styles together and practiced with different weapons. I learned how to conceal them under clothes so humans wouldn't notice them. I spent many nights just thinking hard on how to face him.

In 1987, I was in California. I had gone out to sit on a cliff edge by the ocean. I was going to clear my mind and meditate, instead of practicing that night. I don't know how he found me so fast, as I had just fled from a town in the mid west but he was there.

I was sitting there, legs curled underneath me. My knees were slightly off the edge of the cliff. The spray from the ocean cooling my face helped me as I breathed deep the calming night air. I felt him a moment before he was there.

I started to roll off the cliff thinking a fall would give me time to prepare, but he caught me. He rolled me back so I was away from the edge. We fought across the cliff. I would push him off and flip around. He would lunge and grab, but was not really fighting me.

After just a few minutes he asked if I enjoyed the dance. I struck out at him. He caught my arm like I expected. I pulled him towards me and we fell to the ground. I landed on top of him, one hand holding his neck, the other above his heart.

He lay beneath me smiling. I could feel him waiting. No fighting, just waiting. He closed his eyes, leaned his head up, pushing against my hand at his chest. I did not move, not to push in my hand, not to pull away. I was breathing calmly but my insides were screaming, "Finish Him!"

I had him, and I froze on top of him. I closed my eyes and tried to will my hand into his chest. I felt him move up again, I opened my eyes and he was sniffing me. Inhaling my scent with me so close to him.

"You smell wonderful" He smiled at me. His eyes were filled with lust. He looked like my husband of old. A man who was so in love he could imagine nothing better than to gaze upon me. I felt a twinge in my heart. I felt a tear threaten my eye.

I could not show any emotion or he would think I still wanted him, but I longed to be held again. I sighed and felt all my resolve leave in that sigh. My instincts jumped back on and I moved off him before he could attack me while I was soft.

"Adam I can never go back to that. You've hurt us too much. I don't love you anymore." I felt the tear start to fall, and I fled. I cried into the wind as I flew away from him. I did long to be held, but not by him. I loved him long ago, but not anymore. He was no longer my husband.

I cried.

I wasn't strong enough.

I held his life in my hand.

And he still lives.

If I fail this time, whoever you are reading this, it's up to you. Please be strong and know that he must die. He has lived since the beginning of time, getting more twisted each lifetime.

Chapter 13
Not An Angel

I sit staring at the computer. Was I really done? Was all my life only two nights worth of writing? No, it wasn't. But Adam was not worth much more time than that... From the account sitting in front of me, anyone who read it would know he is the root of all pain here on Earth.

I stand and stretch my arms up and arch my back. The sun was not close to rising yet. I still feel very energetic though which is really weird.

Oh, Derek.

His name whispers through my thoughts.

I had innocent blood tonight. I realize I won't even feel weak when I wake tonight. Well, I might as well go up to the roof, clear my mind and enjoy the night air at least one last time.

After I wake, I can start actively searching for him. I can travel towards him and hunt him for a change. I would pick the battle field this time.

I save the file on both my computer and the little thumb disc thing I don't really understand. I drop the device into a padded envelope and write instructions to open only if my death is felt. I put it in a box and label it for the witch. I put it down on the desk and head out. I can get it and put it in the mail tomorrow before I start after Adam.

As I pull open the door to the roof I feel the cool night air and sigh. I still love the night. He had tried to ruin it for me, but knowing I was not going to kill tonight, I was able to enjoy it. I take off the sweater and pull down my hair.

I sit down on the edge of the roof in my jeans and a white shirt and let a foot dangle down the building. Expending just a little power to hide myself from humans. I didn't need a huge problem if someone sees me and thinks I am going to jump.

I sit for awhile lifting my face to the sky and feeling the wind through my hair. I've learned to enjoy the small moments that I'm lucky enough to get. Where I can just breathe in the air and not worry about anything. I know that the powers I had were part of a curse, but I remember them before they were a curse. I knew I shouldn't like them now, but I still found myself enjoying them from time to time, like this. I was doing nothing really, but I knew I could survive the fall, so I wasn't worried.

Other times I would find myself running as fast as I could across fields just to feel the wind in my hair. Go out sometimes in early morning before the sun rose and jump across the building tops. I would spread my arms and feel nothing around me. It was the most wonderful feeling. Yet when I come to a stop, the feeling of guilt always catches up with me.

These were a curse. I used to be able to do this during the day. I should either have no powers, or not be limited. After I slow down, reality always catches up with me. I was cursed and I was limited.

Tonight however, I feel no guilt in my powers. My story was done. I had trained as much as I possibly could to face him. I would soon rid the world of him, or die trying. Either way, I had done my part. I will make up for my sins at the beginning of time by taking him out of the world.

I feel a pull and realize I shouldn't have thought of him. Especially with my energy running so high out in the open where my energy isn't blocked by so many walls. Just that one thought and my soul reaches out to his. That's the pain with truly being made for someone else. Our spirits are intertwined.

My energy sought his, and found it, close. He has been shielding from me. I was hiding from him. In my fear of being found I had not searched strongly enough. I had let him get close and had confused the dullness of his power for distance, not shielding.

He was in my town.

I jump up to my feet on the edge of the building. I have a split second to hide or go to fight. If I did not chase him down or shield right away, he would find me. Before I can decide, he chose for me.

He sent me the image he could see in a window. It was him standing by the edge of a pool. It was an outdoor pool on the roof of a hotel. Windowed walls surrounded it with an open ceiling. He was holding onto a young girl who was struggling. Her long red hair was almost trailing in the water. He sunk his teeth into her and she screamed as he cut of the vision. He stared at his own eyes, in the window as he sent it, so it looked like he was looking me in the eyes.

I take flight. Running over the building tops with my heart enraged at him anew. I do not know the girl, but she was me. He had been purposely finding girls that looked like me, to feed off of. He never blurs their thoughts or changes their memories. He cannot have me, so he torments me through my children. He knows I see all humans as my children, but the red headed, blue eyed girls he sees as my direct children. A direct link to hurt me with.

I jump from building to building. I stop by the river and sniff the air. I can smell him, and fear. I try to pin point, but have to seek out his energy. I hate doing this because it lets me see through his eyes sometimes, and I so do not want to see what he was doing right now.

No such luck sweet cheeks. I see my face staring up at me screaming. I try to block that out, and see the hotel name on a gym towel with my peripheral. I head to the roof. It was just one bridge down and across the river, I can save her. I have to. I run across the top of the bridge across the river, I *will* get there in time.

I land on the floor at the other end of the pool from him. He's kneeling slightly now, she is laying limp in his arms, still alive, but he has taken the fight out of her. He looks up at me and lifts from her neck. Smirking at me as he slowly stands up tall, holding her loosely in his arm. She tries to move off to the side, tries to fall out of his arms, to somehow get away, but doesn't have the strength.

"Little one. How lovely of you to finally visit me. Are you hungry?" He asks. I don't know why he always acts like we're old friends. It didn't torment me, it didn't piss me off. It was as if he thought I was just in a bad mood, a female spell, and one day would just come back to him. I will never understand him, but I don't want to.

Today however, he asks just to spite me. He holds her limp body out to me, as if offering to share, although I can sense he has bled her almost dry.

"I'm not visiting Adam. I'm here for her" I point to the child. I never take my eyes off him, just a motion of my hand. She shrinks away from me and my words. I ignore it. Losing to him now, due to my pity for her, would not save her.

"She doesn't want you. See her come back to me." He flashes his teeth at me then lets her limp body fall to the ground. I see her try to move away and fail again. She may be almost dead and frightened half way insane, but she's still fighting, I like her.

His eyes slither over me before he looks meets my eyes and his smirk turns into a full smile.

"You've fed well tonight haven't you? Not your usual feeding. You did not take from many tonight." He closes his eyes and sniffs the air. I feel his power roll over me slightly and do not flinch. I will never let him use fear against me ever again. I'm all grown up now, how about that.

He finishes tasting my energy and sighs as he opens his eyes wide at me. "A male but not your usual prey. Ah. You have decided to come back to me."

I stand straight and brace myself, He was in a good mood, and I was about to break it big time. I have to get rid of him fast or she would be lost and so would I.

"Do not torment yourself with thoughts of touching me again. Adam. I will never be yours again" His entire demeanor changes so fast that I almost miss it. He glares at me, no longer trying with any pretenses and lets his full anger flow out of him.

"Your own children cower from you. I love you for you. I know you, and will always know you. My little one, stop running. Do not fight me anymore. You waste your energy on these ungrateful brats" he motions his hand towards the dying girl at his feet. The child whimpers and tries to shy away again. His anger was all for me though.

She was just a toy to him. No child to him. He saw food. But he knew I saw her as my own, and he used that. His face turns pleading and his voice melodic, but the days where I could be swayed by him are long gone.

"Why do you not come back to me, so you can be loved for you? Together, we could make it so they knew you as Mother. They could love you as well"

"Adam, I know you as well. I know how you would have them see me." I try to side step closer, hoping he would move to oppose me. I step back as he stands firm and just follows with his eyes.

"It matters not how they learn. They will know you as Mother, and I know you long to be a mother again." He smirks at me and I hide the anger.

The urge to rush him pulls at me muscles but I have to stay calm. Being a mother was the only thing that ever made me happy when we were first cursed. As a mortal it was one of the most wonderful things I had felt. He took both away from me. He knows it hurts me. It has lessened since my changing, but he can still make it feel fresh it seems.

"There is only One Mother, Adam. I am not her, and you know it. You just ignore her, because you cannot face that your betrayal has made you what you are." His power fills the air, even the water ripples as his anger grows. The girl curls tighter and cries softly. He glances down at the noise.

He had forgotten about her, which saved her life until now. He would kill her to spite me so I keep his attention on me. I lean to one side and trail my fingers along my hip.

"Adam." I say it with a hidden compulsion in the word to make him look, "you do this to yourself. As you have always done things that harm you. You lost your mother. You lost your children. Your life." I pause but before I speak the last kicker of my little speak. He sneers at me and interrupts with a smug filled voice.

"She is long gone. Even if she does exist somewhere, old and decrepit, she no longer cares for me. So why should I worship Her, when her own foolishness has made me a God?" He stares at me like he has made the ultimate point and I could not disagree with him.

"You've even lost your wife." I finish as if he had never spoken. I raise my eyebrow and lick my lips as I start a laughing smile, "When will you finally let you see all this and give up?" I do not look away but I show him that I do not fear him with a condescending look. I mask the fear I hold for the girl as I feel her life grow faint.

"I will not give up, you are mine!" He launches at me. I don't want to fight because in the time it took for one of us to win, she will die. I flinch to the side in an attempt to drive a solid hit into his side but he was gone. He had flown up and over the wall. He was gone, no power, no form, nothing.

I don't want to wait for him to return. I run over to the young girl. She begins shying away from me as much as she can. I bend down to pick her up, touching her shoulders with my fingers to unroll her from the tight ball she'd made with her body.

"No." she whispers. I can feel it was supposed to be a yell but she hadn't the strength. "Please, no more." She said.

I look in her heart and see that she thinks I will do as he has done. Worse than that, however, she has given up on life.

She was asking that I not feed and that she not live. To me and to no one she begged for her life and for it to end. She has seen the devil and does not want to live in the painful world that allows him to exist anymore. I cry inside for her and know I have to save her. Body and spirit.

I focus my energy and blur her mind. I calm down the turbulence in her thoughts and send an image around me. She looks up and sees me in a flowing white gown and light surrounding me. I speak in her mind instead of out loud, to help her feel like it is truly a spiritual moment.

My child, you shall not die. I will help you. For you have faced darkness, and won.

She reaches out for me and I take flight with her in my arms. I keep her mind held so she feels calm. I try to hold her life to her and try to keep her from giving up. The drain starts to make me feel light headed. It would have been so much easier to hold her mind if I had a blood link to her, but she was empty.

I drop her off at the hospital a few city blocks away. I plant an image in her mind of a man, and a fight. It's the best I can do without taking her blood. I cannot make her completely new memories, but I can fog and manipulate the ones she already has. She will not remember Adam. She will not remember him feeding.

She will have traumatic amnesia and never fully remember anything from this night. She will always feel that she was saved from darkness this night, and be thankful. I send a mental urge to the staff and leave her on the bench outside. I feel a nurse come outside and fly off.

"An angel brought me here" I hear the girl say before she faints in the arms of the nurse. I start off again, faster then I normally allow myself. I am feeling weak. I need to get home and get to rest before the sun is even close to rising.

"I thank you Derek. Without your blood I may not have been able to save her." I say aloud to no one.

'She shied away from me' echoed through my thoughts. There was no more blood to take. Without his blood I could not have changed her memories and she would not have let me save her. How many other innocents could I have saved from Adam if I had been stronger all these years?

I try not to think of that as I land on my building, but it stays with me. I can't change anything now. He knows I'm here. And he is angry. I need to rest.

Chapter 14
Night in the Park

I wake as the sun is leaving the sky. Derek's blood should have woken me with extraordinary strength, but I had expended much energy to save a girl I could not drink from. I was stronger then I normally would have been just waking, but not as strong as I could have been. One taste of her blood and it would have been easy to hold her mind and save her, but Adam had made sure I could not.

I realize now, that he had intended to leave her, but when I showed up he made sure I had to choose. Chase him, or save her. He knew I could not drink from her, and if I choose to save her I would waste energy, weakening myself for tonight. I had played right into his hands.

"It will end tonight. I promise you." I say to the mirror. I pull my hair up into a high ponytail, and do something I had not done in years.

"Mother, help us tonight. I, your forsaken daughter, ask nothing for myself. I ask only that after tonight your other children will have a better life. If I must die to ensure that, I shall with a happy heart. I only pray that he will die with me." I close my eyes and take a deep breath.

I prepare myself with my knives in my sleeves. I have a small dagger on one leg, and a hand gun at the small of my back. If it comes down to me using the gun, then I have probably already lost. It may slow him down just long enough for me to kill us both, but I know that I had to finish this tonight. I'm taking all my toys just in case. I grab the box with my life story hidden inside.

I ignore my jacket as I walk out of the apartment. I won't need it for heat, and I'm not hiding anymore. I head down the stairs. I am not dreading anything, but feel no need to rush to him. I place my package in the building mail box and head out into the night.

As I walk outside I hear someone in the alley beside my building. One hushed voice very forceful, and another very calm voice with a high heart rate. I do not have to hunt my dinner this night, and for once, I do not regret it.

Looking down the alley I see a man being mugged by a boy no more than twenty five years. There is only the two of them. The man is calm even though the knife is on his throat, or maybe because of it. I hear the younger man threaten his elder as he takes the wallet.

"And your watch to old man, I want that." He tries to put the wallet in his own jacket pocket while holding the knife on his victim.

I blur the older man's mind so he won't see me. I step up to the side of the boy and grab his hand. He stares at me a little afraid.

Not like others are afraid though. He is not afraid of me, he is afraid of death. He knows he has been caught, and fears punishment. I pull him back and my strength gives him the fear of me that I know so well. He reaches in his pocket and throws the wallet at the elder man.

"Here man, take it back." He tries to do the right thing, but he can't change it. It is already in his body. Even if he was pure, he is now tainted and I can feed. The older man grabs his wallet and heads down the alley. He turns at the end and shakes his head before leaving.

I look in his mind and see that he does not intend to turn the young man in, he saw the boy get scared, but not me. He believes the kid came to his senses and let him go due to an attack of conscience. As he leaves sight, I use my small knife to cut the boy's neck.

I feed a little more then I normally do from one victim, but I will need strength tonight. I let him down softly. He will remember trying to mug a man, getting scared. That he froze up before that man hit him and ran. He will be too embarrassed to say anything to anyone. Hopefully he will not attempt this again. I lay him down next to the dumpster and leave.

I blur my image and run a few blocks away. I feed again from a man who was trying to break into an apartment from the fire escape. I feed on him quickly and leave him on the stairs thinking he had slipped on the window sill.

With two meals I was refreshed. The power from Derek last night had not yet run completely out. Helping the girl had drained me, but not completely. The power was still in me. I had forgotten now much innocent blood could fill me.

I set out into the city. I can't search for his energy because he will feel me. I had to do this without our connection. I smell the air and catch nothing.

He won't be in my part of town. I realize he wants pure blood and there is none of that here. Someone he can scare and torment. I turn around and head to the river.

I just know he will be across it, in a nice part of town. He's not just feeding. He is not simply hunting. He is searching for someone whose blood calls to him. For someone so low, he has high tastes.

After I get across the bridge, I turn to the nicer parts of town. I know somewhere he is hunting, and if I want to win, I need to find him soon.

I catch his scent. As I start to track it I feel his power. I do not search him out with my mind, but use my physical senses to find him. I get a rush and feel his strength nearby and I smile and speed up. I was no longer caring about stealth or surprise, though they would still help.

He has not fed yet.

He's sitting on a bench, right inside the fences of City Center. The walk through park had a small pond for ducks that was used during migration. The whole park was planted for that purpose, but was used mostly for those of the upper class to feel like they were not in a big city.

I sense no one else in the park at the moment. I hide myself from view, and my power from him. I calm myself and felt again. No, he had not fed yet. I still have Derek's blood and two meals tonight. I may have a chance, but I have to hurry.

He stands up. I look to where his eyes prowl, and see why he was waiting. There is a theater down the street, and patrons are leaving. The play must be over, and he expects to take someone away from a pleasant evening. Not this night big bad wolf.

I race over, get in between him and the theater and stop in his path. He stops his slow walk and stares at me. Hatred in his eyes, and behind them, I saw the surprise he was recovering from.

Oh yay, I like being the cat so much better than the mouse.

"Hello Adam." I put my right foot behind me at an angle and look at him slightly over my left shoulder. My fingers moving slightly as I wait for his response. I'm trying to keep them loose and ready but they itch for a knife. He stands there and does not move, but stares at me with putrid bile in his gaze.

"That's not my name." he finally said. It felt like it had been an hour, when in reality it had only been seconds.

"It's how the world knows you. And what I will call you." I reply as I stand up straight.

"You will learn respect. Wife. You will finally know your place. I have let you play this silly game too long. Come back now and I will be. Pleasant. Resist again and I will see to it that you remember your place."

"I know my place. Adam, learn yours"

We both launch at the same time. I slip to the left, but reach my right arm out. As he flies past I grab at his shoulder and pull him around. He is only slightly slower than normal. Even with extra feedings I am barely faster.

126

He lands and turns to face me, I am still holding in my power. I do not want him to know how much I have until I am ready. He rushes me again, this time I know he will make contact, so I start to fall backwards. He lands on me and I roll backwards kicking with both feet in his belly, throwing him past me. If I can get us to the middle of the park, then I can stop using power to hide us and can focus on finally dispensing the world of him.

I launch myself straight at him, using power to speed me up and pushing the rest into him. I feel him push back with his own and I see him brace for an attack. He has split his energy between a long sharp blade to cut through my defenses, and a curved wall around him to stop me from attack.

"Aw did I scare you?" I yell as I side step around the blade of power unseen in the air and head straight for his shielded wall.

He puts a leg back and braces for me to fall in front of him and change tactics. He never was good at reading people. I surge power below me and flip over, landing behind him. I don't try to land standing and fight. I fall and turn sweeping out his legs at his ankles. He starts to fall sideways but turns his upper body and lands on his hands. I roll back and further away from the humans.

He runs at me, holding back his power. I know he intends to hit me with everything at once and jump straight up as he nears me. I kick back and land a solid hit on his upper back. He tries to recover but his momentum and my kick send him to the ground.

He tries to jump up, but in his anger doesn't notice me on the left side of him now. I grab his arm and throw him behind me, further into the park.

I chase after him. No one can see us now. We are far enough in that I can now fight with full force and power. I don't have to hide us, and I can kill without worry of being seen.

He is already standing when I get to him. I stop a mere ten feet in front of him. He is snarling with a drop of blood on his lip. I feel his anger permeate my skin as he glares at me. I know that this time, if I fail to kill him, he will never let me go.

"I am going to have to kill you Sa'ara. You will be reborn so it doesn't matter. I will find you, change you again. This time teach you proper respect. I will not allow you the freedoms that you received this lifetime." He threw all his power at me and I shielded at the last second. As soon as I feel it deflect I threw mine back at him with a throwing knife at the tip. Flying in the exact path his attack had cleared in his defenses, it struck home in his shoulder. He stumbled a little to the side.

"You're getting slow old man." He started to run at me.

I fell to the ground as he jumped at me. I grabbed his legs and used him to flip over and land away from him again. He lands on his knees and one hand, staring up at me. Loathing me for what I'd become, but in his eyes I saw that he still hesitated to kill me.

I taste his energy, thinking about that hesitation and instantly knew what he didn't like to feel. He knew that he was evil, and somewhere, he still feared the Mother. If I killed him, then he would have to face her judgment on what he had become.

"Could you live through a second curse Adam?" I asked aloud without thinking. Outraged, he howled.

I heard more pain and hatred then I knew one being could have in that scream and he flew at me from the ground. I wasn't prepared and fell back on the ground. He landed on me and I was stuck. My gun pressed into the ground under my back and was sealed off. I try flipping him off with my legs but his force had pushed his knees into the ground beside me. He presses me down into the soft dirt with his body and power. His knees pinning my thighs, his feet curved over to hold mine down. He sits on my waist and grabs my wrists. Pulling my arms above my head he glares at me an inch from my face. Our noses touched lightly and I shivered.

He had not liked me knowing his own thoughts. He never admitted fears to himself, but I had spoken them aloud. His self loathing, fear, and hatred of himself gave him more power then I knew either of us had.

"I told you to show respect. I could have let you rot with the rest of them. I gave you life and you spit it back at me!" He pushes my hands deeper into the ground, my elbows bent to the point of pain. He moved to hold them with one hand. The other he trailed down my arm. He paused slightly as he touched the knife against it and glared at me.

"In your next life, you will know nothing, but me. I will make sure of it." His hand reached my shoulder and moved to the front of me. Touching my collarbone lightly before he trailed his fingers across my chest and rested above my heart.

"You will behave." He said caressing my breast. I fight with everything I was not to spit in his face. I will not let him take me again. If I can just get to my gun I can make sure he never hurts anyone with that again. I need to calm him down enough to move my hands.

"I will make sure that next time, you will not remember anything of your previous lives!" I feel his fingers start to push through my skin and realize I was wrong about his intentions.

I thought he was going to try and rape me one last time before he killed me. I was wrong. He wasn't going to risk me escaping again. He was opening my chest, and was going to take out my heart.

I have failed, and am going to die because I am not fast enough. How long till I am reborn? How much stronger will he get?

"Adamah"

I hear myself whisper his name.

His hand paused then he froze completely. He was not letting me up, he was not leaving, but at least his hand was not pushing further into me. His eyes look up into mine slowly, cautiously. I remember that he had not heard his name since my first death.

He looks at me, waiting, wanting, a look I had seen in Fredrick's eyes. The thought of him put love in my eyes, I feel it. He sees it. The man, who is on the verge of killing me, has hope. Seeing love in my eyes he thinks is for him. Hopes are for him. I might still succeed tonight.

Just a change of tactics girl. You can do this

"I am so sorry. I see now that you are hurting because of me." I feel his power level shrink like a sigh as I look straight in his eyes.

"I can see now. All you ever wanted was me. For me to be beside you. To stay beside you. I am so sorry I put you through this." I say the last sincerely. I truly am sorry he had to go through hell. But it was his own fault and I am also sorry I have to kill him. I was sorry we had come to this.

"I knew you still loved me. I knew someday, you would remember me." The anger in his eyes fades even as I watch. He looks at me with his version of love. He would have a companion again, no longer be alone.

I see all this in his eyes, but know he was lying. To himself more then to me. He does not love me. He just loves the idea of never being alone again. When we were first together, he had loved me. I know that now he is no longer capable of true love.   He is too twisted from years alone, and will never be the same. He could remember love, but his days of true compassion were over long ago. I did not want to be like him in any way, but to defeat him. I have to trick him.

He leans in and inhales my scent. Rubs his face across my cheek. I press my cheek back against his. I know what he wants, and I can use that. As he lifts his head back up, I look up into his eyes. Inhaling sharply I open my mouth, and sigh. I stretch my body out underneath his and see a new emotion in his eyes. That's what I'm looking for.

He knows my body. I may have been reborn a human, but my body was still the same form it had been before. My soul kept the form it knew. A form that was made for him. No one else could make him feel like I could. No other body would please him as mine could. We both know it.

He leans in and kisses me. Surprisingly tender and soft coming from him. I kiss him back. The hand that had stopped its assault towards my heart was now splayed out across my chest. He moves upward, retracing the steps his hand had taken down my arm from before, but enjoying it this time. He is not keeping me pinned to death or fighting for his life he thinks. He is finally able to touch me without rejection. To feel the simplicity of pure pleasure.

It is not hard for me to fake acceptance of him. Sadly, as I was made for him, so he was for me. Even as I am repulsed, my body reacts. When he is proper and careful, no body but his can give me perfect pleasure. I truly do feel for him.

It is easy to be with him when he is so needful. I know though, that when he is appeased, he will be Adam again. I have love, true Soul mate love for Adamah, but I could never love the man he had become.

That thought alone keeps me from running.

That thought keeps me going.

He had not only killed Fredrick, my mortal husband, this man was also the death of my soul mate.

While I had been thinking about all this, he kept going. He had let go of my hands and even pulled them out of the ground for me. He had one hand behind my neck. He was kissing my neck, and there was nothing vampirish about it. Anyone could walk by right now and think we were a couple of kids. His other hand is on my waist. Fingers tickling at my jeans.

It seems hearing his name brought back the spark of my first love. He is not craving violence. He does not want fear. He wants me. Which made what I have to do all the harder.

I reach up with one hand and touch his cheek. He freezes, until I smile. He relaxes against me. I reach up and kiss him of my own accord. I feel tears hiding in the corners of my eyes. Memories flash behind my eyes.

I remember sitting with Adamah on the shore. Holding him as the waves tickled our feet. I taste the first blood that had begun this curse. I see our first child, my pure beautiful daughter. I remember dying and waking with a hunger seeing my own children.

I cry out softly as I kiss him. I relive breaking the flesh of my son's neck with teeth before I can stop the memory. Adam groans slightly and brings me back to the present.

Come on girl keep your head have to stay focused.

I pull his head down towards me. One hand on the back of his head, the other trailing fingertips at his cheek. He bends down and kisses me deeply. I open my lips to his. His hand makes its way to my thighs and pulls me up towards him. I move my hand from his head and slide it down his back as I pull one of my legs out from under him. He moves to the side to allow the movement, then moves between my legs instead of lying on top of them.

I keep my true thoughts to myself and put false thoughts to the front of my mind. If he touches my mind he will believe I am sincere. This isn't hard because I kind of am, at least my hormones am. My body is on fire at his fingertips, my soul screaming for his. I try to keep my mind set on the task. Memories were flooding me again. I was getting flashes, my body trying to stay in the moment as my mind fights for control.

I see us before the curse, feel him inside me. I cried out in pleasure in the memory and against his mouth on the ground now. He swallows down my moans and feeds me his own. I pull my mouth back to breathe. His mouth moves to my neck as his hands find my lower back and chest.

Girl, calm your body down or you'll never get through this.

I pull up memories that were not of my true love, not my soul mate, but the creature it had become. I pull on the memories of him torturing me after my change, the women he tortured in front of me.

"Adamah" I whisper into his hair and felt a tear escape my eye. I miss him, but he was long gone. The feelings are a trick, this was not my love. He leans up and looks at me.

"Do not cry Sa'ara. We will never be apart again." he lifts me up, leaving behind all promise of sex, and hugs me. I am stunned, and begin crying. He cannot show me any nicety or I might give in.

No Tamson, remember this isn't him.

"I am so sorry Adamah. I don't know what went wrong." I cry into his shoulder as he pulls me in closer. I feel my shoulder moisten and realize he too is crying.

"I don't know either Sa'ara. We can forget it though. We can start over. Nothing is impossible now that we are together again." He smiles at me and kisses my lips chastely before returning his head to my shoulder and squeezing me lovingly.

I close my eyes. Hearing his name had brought him back to me. I could smell the difference. The person holding me, the man I held to me right now, was Adamah. My soul mate, untainted. But I can also sense Adam. Lurking in the shadows. He will return. He did not like being pushed aside. I take a deep breath.

Now or never Tamson, finish this

I sigh aloud and squeeze him back. I move my hands to his chest and push lightly. He lets me lift him up. His hands on the ground beside me he simply looks at me with happy curiosity.

"I love you, Adamah. I always have." I say truthfully. Grateful that I get to say it.

"I love you as well Sa'ara" he says and starts to lean down for a kiss.

As he moves forward I push into his chest with my right hand, and rip out his heart. I push up with my left hand on his shoulder so he falls to the side, and I roll away from him. I see surprise, and sorrow on his face before Adams with hatred rolls forward. Seeing Adam helps me keep calm while my heart screams in agony at having to kill him.

"I am truly sorry that it came to this Adam. I am sorry I let you drink the blood. I am sorry that I died and left you alone. I am sorry that you had to be alone for so long and that you became the twisted and evil thing before me. I am sorry that I could not stop all of this, but I am not sorry that I can give you this." I step back as he tries to crawl towards me. I feel tears slide down my cheeks as my fingers tighten on his heart.

"I am giving you a gift you didn't give me Adam. I'm letting you die, and I will not bring you back." His eyes open wide as I crush his heart in my hand. I call a power I haven't used in ages. I feel heat grow in my body. My bones warming then burning and pulling it out through my muscles and send it out to the mass in my hand.

His throat gurgles as his heart bursts into flames; he begins to scramble towards me. Before he gets far his hand begins to decay in front of his face.

He stares as the decay spreads down his arm. He looks up at me right as the decay reaches his face.

I sob as I watch his decayed body start turning to ash on the same path. For a moment he is still there. I stare at the ash sculpture that looks like it could forever crawl and beg in hatred. I feel another tear fall for the empty shell of the body that had once been my other half.

I call up wind and close my eyes as he is taken away from me. I open my eyes after a moment and let the wind die down. I look around at our battlefield that was almost my deathbed and see blood everywhere. I pull up the heat and touch each drop I can see. Closing my eyes I reach out and sense drops in the dirt I cannot see or hidden in grass. If I want to rid the world of him, I have to get everything. I cry as each drop sizzles and disappears. For once I am able to use my power over the world, and not feel wrong about them. I find the final drop and hesitate. I wipe the tear from my cheeks and stare at it.

My soul mate. My first love. A being made just to be with me. Am I really the cause of all his pain?

Not really and you know it so stop stalling.

I know deep down that we were both tempted equally, and I just fought it off better. Once he started thinking there was nothing I could have done.

Was there though?

It doesn't matter now. He had chosen his path, and it ended with me and this one drop.

I take a deep breath. Call upon the fire one last time, and watch the last remnant of him turn to smoke.

I start to stand up and freeze. I can feel the ache in my chest that I normally ignore. The pain and emptiness that I had felt the entire time of our curse feels stronger somehow. My eyes close as that ache grew.

Without his body and soul on the world, nothing was here to feel his pain.

My soul is taking on the full burden of the curse? I scream out as the pain becomes unbearable. I feel my powers growing. I could do anything. I lie down and begin sobbing again but there are no tears, just howls as pain rakes through my every cell. I have finally ridden the world of his presence, but I might not be able to survive his death.

Is this pain what he felt? Could I also become evil and twisted? I realize that maybe he had no choice. If he had felt this pain upon my death, maybe feeding off others pain lessened this feeling.

"I don't want to become him." I whisper into the ground. I close my eyes as it grows even more intense. I feel for Adam now. Feel for him not Adamah, because if he was born of this pain, no wonder he was so twisted.

At least you stopped him, girl. At least you stopped this pain for him.

As I lay there staring into nothing and realize that the pain had stopped increasing. My whole body feels like it has been hollowed out and filled by sorrow. It feels like I'm just one big body of hurt.

Chapter 15
A Vampire Reborn

I don't know how long I've been here. I stopped thinking about the pain a while ago. I blink and realize that dawn is coming. I can feel it more now than before. I know how much it would hurt if I stayed here, but a part of me wants to.

I want to die. I do not want to become a twisted version of myself.

I would grow as he had and spread evil in a world I had just tried to save. I'll stay here, close my eyes and will myself to stay still when the rays of light touch me.

As dawn creeps closer I turn my head towards it, but pain does not echo through my muscles. I take a breath and my chest doesn't cringe in pain. I stand up staring at my hands. I feel less each second. I close my eyes, feeling it lessen faster and faster.

My pain is leaving. The emptiness filling. I slam my eyes shut against fresh tears as I realize the pain is less then I had felt before I killed him. I focus and really remember what it felt like before. My breath speeds up as the pain recedes even more and begin to disappear.

I feel the hollowness inside me fill up. I pinch my eyes closer together, hoping beyond hope that this was not a trick, when I feel a stirring. I hold my breath and reach for that stirring in my mind.

I calm everything down and feel that ripple grow closer to me. I hear a whisper of sound reach me as the first tear falls from my eyes. I dare not move for fear the movement would push back at the ripple and bring back the pain. I feel a stronger whisper in my ears, a sigh.

It feels like when Adam spoke to me at my debut. I feel the breath without a person near me. Only this time I know the speaker, I know I will not see her.

"My child." brushes across my mind and I almost fall to my knees. I cry silent tears as the voice of my mother fills my mind and erases the pain completely.

"You have lived long. Suffered much. You have spent your entire lifetime trying to protect your children. My children. Even in your moments of pain, you thought of them. Your self imposed penance should be lifted now child. I have a task for you." I feel her hands upon me, though I know she is not here. Invisible hands lift me to stand before her.

"You took this lifetime to destroy him. To cleanse my world of him. You weakened yourself in the process. You only fed from those who would only sustain you, never did you allow yourself to be fulfilled and nourished properly. Yet you still sought to free the world of him. I have watched you and learned that I cannot let another grow to be like him." I feel her sigh at the thought of him. The knowledge fills me that she knows it was her fault.

That the suffering that he caused went back to the punishment she bestowed upon us. She knows this and has despaired with her children.

"You have cleansed the world of his body, but he still lives. He has made vampire children, and he has tainted his human children. His evil is spread around the world, but so is your light." The warmth of a smile spreads over my skin as she beams at me. "You have also touched your human children and helped. Now, I need your light."

I feel her hands hold mine and I lift them in front of me. I see an image of her hands touching mine, mirroring them.

"Be my hand on earth. Use all your abilities. They are my gifts to you once again. You are no longer cursed my child. I cannot take away your night and blood life, that is part of you now, and you will need it to fight what he has done. I can lessen it and I can give this to you. You will now be the only vampire with my presence. I will always be with you. You will no longer bring instinctual fear to humans. You may walk amongst them and be close to your children once again. With my presence, you will also be harder for his children to sense."

My hands grow hot, and light. I feel her power move through my arms and fill my chest. I breathe in her scent and hold it with me.

"You will know when one of his is near, because you will not sense me. I am in everything, except them. You must rid the world of his children before he is truly gone." I resist the urge to reach out and hold on when I feel her hands leave mine. I feel the ripple pulling away. I have been without her for so long I am afraid of her leaving again.

"Go now, do my bidding, and suffer no more." She was gone, but she wasn't. The ripple is gone, the breath has faded away. She was no longer beside me, but she is inside me once again. I open my eyes and saw the sky had lightened a little. I swallow and exhale. There is no pain, no emptiness, and no sorrow. Looking over my body I see my wounds from the fight are gone.

I start laughing as I hug myself, and walk out of the park. As I reached the entrance to the park a couple walks past me. They smile, the man nods and they walk on.

I haven't been smiled at in years. Not by someone who wasn't under my mind spell. I watch them walk away grateful for a present they didn't know they had given me. They hadn't looked at me and ducked away without knowing why I made them uncomfortable.

I will still have to feed from my own children, and live in the darkness, but I will be accepted. I walk home slowly. I say hi to a few people in my neighborhood. I rejoice inwardly that they are no longer in danger knowing me.

After lifetimes and years of hiding, your free girl, never thought you'd see that huh?

I get home and see my computer still waiting. I walk over and sit in front of it, touching the keys. I had purchased it in case I failed. But I had not.

You won.

I smile and sigh happily. There is still an hour before true sunrise. I had not had free time in over a century. I have been running, hiding, and training.

I turned on the computer and look over the file of my life. I almost delete it.

Almost.

I want to keep it.

I will always keep it. It can help me retrace my own footsteps, and maybe find his. I was going to be the Hunter now. Not tonight, but I have to start somewhere. I pick up the picture of Father, mother and myself.

"I want to go home" I say aloud and touch a finger to them. I put the picture down. I pull up a webpage to buy plane tickets. I am going to relax, and travel like a normal person for once. I buy a ticket that leaves two nights from now and go to sleep.

I wake and pack my bag. I go out to eat and visit a bar. I go in and talk without shame. I am even invited back to a few places. I finally go with one gentleman back to his apartment. He had not been drinking, for he was driving for his friends so they could drink. I sit in the passenger seat and we talk as he drove them all home.

Then we head to his home. He asks if I wanted a drink, then we watch a movie, about vampires ironically, on his T.V.

Wow not only did they mess up Adam and Eve, they got us wrong once again. But it keeps making me laugh.

I'm so excited about having a normal night, I almost forget to eat. He had been expecting sex. I know I can't really give it to him. It is too personal to me. So as the movie end I reach up and hug him. I kiss his neck as he pulls me closer. I take over his mind, and he falls asleep.

I place in him the memories he will wake with. A wild night that he will be able to replay whenever he wants. I make sure to implant every detail for him, so he will be able to recollect everything. I'll give him this wonderful night as my present to him.

He did nothing great that he knew of, but he is my first meal without remorse. I take what I need and get up.

I remember that I have more power now and that with the goddess within me again I may have some of my original abilities back. I touch his cheek and close my eyes. As I picture the white light that she had put in my hands I feel my fingertips and his skin grow warm.

I open my eyes and he's healed. A smile plays on my lips as I leave a small note thanking him for a wonderful night. At home I pack up the apartment with a note of donation to the poor. Turn in my last month's rent, and key. Leave a note to the landlord thanking him for the apartment, but that I had family trouble and had to fly back home and would be staying.

The next night I wake, grab my bag, and race to the airport. Since I no longer need to feel ashamed at my powers I can finally run and fly as fast as I can and enjoy it.

The airline will take me back over the ocean and have me there with time to hide before the sun rose. I purchased a coach ticket. I want to see and be with humans. I want to be in their world for once.

Almost everyone falls asleep soon after we take off. There's a young man with a backpack near the back who sang quietly at his window. A mother hums as she holds her child in her lap near the front. Near the end of the flight a man from the business class section comes to coach and asks the steward if he could walk around because he's bored.

He sees me awake and smiles. He walks over to ask if he can sit with me. We chat a bit until he is asked to return to his seat for landing.

"Thank you for your company, I hope you enjoy your trip." He reaches for my hand and kisses it.

"Thank you for your company, and I wish you well on your return home." I feel myself blush as he walks away. I stare out the window with an excited grin as we land.

I get a room at a hotel nearby. I can travel by foot tomorrow night. It would only take one night. I can go find the Witch, see how my family has turned out.

I put the do not disturb on the door. Lock it, and close the curtains. Taking the blanket off the bed I staple it around the edges of the window.

Just in case, besides I don't need it to stay warm huh.

I put towels at the crack of the door so no hallway sunshine could sneak into the room. I lay down in the bed, amazed that so many people had interacted with me with still no fear set it them, and I fall asleep with a smile.

I wake early. Still not hungry yet. It feels like I should eat, but I'm not starving. I gather my things, and leave using the quick checkout card in my room. I take the stairs up to the roof. Put my bag down before stretching. It feels good to be back. The smells of the city fill me and I giggle.

I grab my bag, put the strap around my shoulder and sit it on my lower back. Then run to the edge and jump into the air. It feels more like floating then flying as I leave the world behind me. I land outside the city and jog.

I blur my image as I pass towns and villages. I stop when I see a farm. It is one of the properties that Fredrick had owned. I know them all by heart even now. I feel the fence post and think of when he had brought me out to see some of the lands. This one was not far from our home. I look up and see the city I had been born in. I walk the rest of the way. The witch's home should be just on the other side of the main housing section. Hidden in the farm and forest lands near the sea.

The joy I had felt living like a normal being slowly disappeared as I walked closer. I reach the city and feel almost depressed. I look around and nothing is the same as I remembered. I know the streets, I see buildings, but it was not right. Something just feels... Off.

I get to the house Father had owned. Baron is still written on the front gates and an elaborate 'B' was new on the front doors. I hold the front gates and stare up at the home.

Is this still my family's house?

Were they ever even really mine?

My soul had made my body; I was just born of them. My thoughts wander as I walk toward where the Godefrey estate had been. I feel dread in my stomach as I get closer.

I haven't been here in almost a century; do I really want to see what it had become?

I get to the house I had once been the lady of. The house where my suffering began and my happiness had once been everything.

I look up at it and feel.... nothing.

I feel my emotions, missed up as they are. But I get nothing from the house.

I can hear life inside. Hearts beat and breathes were being taken. It is as if everything was there and nothing was there.

"Oh no." I whisper into the night. I don't want to believe it. I had thought to come home to catch up and take a break from him.

"You beat me here though didn't you Adam" I say aloud to the house. I leave the house, and am at the Witch's front door in moments.

She answers the door and stares at me in shock.

"I didn't sense you, how did you get so close? When did you get here? Come in, Come in." She ushers me in and grabs my bag.

"What has happened? Is he after you?"

"He is dead. I killed him two nights ago." I sit down and stare up at her.

"Then why do you look so down? Shouldn't we be jumping for joy?" I look up at her and feel tears again.

Won't I ever stop crying? Shouldn't I be dry by now?

"I have much to tell you, and much to do still." I sigh and tell her what had happened. How he had almost killed me, how I finally killed him. I spoke to her of the goddess visiting me, as I stare out the window.

"I came home to relax. Find out about my family before I started out on my task." I finish. She smiles at me, but it fades quickly. She looks at me confused.

"That's wonderful though. You no longer have to hide. Tamson this is amazing, why do you look so sad?" I stare up at her. I don't know how to explain the void I felt inside my old house.

"Did Evelynne have any children? Do I have any family left?" Maybe if it's not my family it won't be so bad.

"Yes, of course! I have kept track of everything. I knew you'd come back, although I did not think it would be so soon. Here let me get everything" She goes to get up.

"No don't" she stops and stares at me quizzically. "That's not what I need right now." What do I want?

"Where does my family live?" I final settle on asking.

"In the same house actually. There's only one left, she was an only child. And both her parents have died. She is engaged though, so hopefully there will be children soon.' She answers happily. I think she is trying to lift my mood. I turn to look out the window.

"What's wrong? Are you not happy? Your family survived!" She kneels in front of me. Eyes searching trying to comprehend what could possibly bother me.

"He has touched the house. I don't know how, but his evil is still there" I hear her gasp but do not turn to her.

"I want to go rest. It will be daylight soon, and I need to start hunting tomorrow."